JUN   1994

The Five-Dollar Smile

AND OTHER STORIES

By the Same Author

The Five-Dollar Smile

AND OTHER STORIES

SHASHI THAROOR

T3683FI

ARCADE PUBLISHING • NEW YORK

FIRST NORTH AMERICAN EDITION

The characters and events in this book are fictitious. Any similarity to real persons, living or dead, is coincidental and not intended by the author.

The stories in this collection were first published in the following magazines: "The Five-Dollar Smile" (*The Illustrated Weekly of India, Chicago Review*); "The Boutique" (*JS*); "How Bobby Chatterjee Turned To Drink" (*Eve's Weekly*); "The Village Girl" (*Eve's Weekly*); "The Temple Thief" (*JS*); "The Simple Man" (*JS*); "The Professor's Daughter" (*The Illustrated Weekly of India*); "Friends" (this story was published as "The Synergists" in *JS*); "The Pyre" (*Youth Times*); "The Political Murder" (*Gentleman*); "Auntie Rita" (*Eve's Weekly*); "The Other Man" (*Eve's Weekly*); "The Solitude of the Short-Story Writer" (*New Review, Cosmopolitan, The Illustrated Weekly of India, The Portable Lower East Side*); "The Death of a Schoolmaster" (*The Illustrated Weekly of India, Discovery*).

Library of Congress Cataloging-in-Publication Data

Tharoor, Shashi, 1956–
    The five-dollar smile and other stories / Shashi Tharoor.—1st
North American ed.
        p.   cm.
    ISBN 1-55970-225-7
    1. India—Fiction.   I. Title.
PR9499.3.T535F5   1993
823—dc20   93-12022

Published in the United States by Arcade Publishing, Inc., New York
Distributed by Little, Brown and Company

10   9   8   7   6   5   4   3   2   1

BP

PRINTED IN THE UNITED STATES OF AMERICA

To my father

CHANDRAN THAROOR

the first reader of many of these stories,
who saw the potential in the scribblings of
a difficult child and did everything possible
to nurture it—this book is offered
with love and gratitude

Contents

Foreword

Since the publication of *The Great Indian Novel* and *Show Business*, I have been asked many times, by a wide variety of people—ranging from an interviewer from Canada to a student at Wellesley College (not to mention a smattering of former readers of Indian magazines now living in this country)—about my earlier stories. Their interest has tempted me to make these pieces available to a new readership.

The stories collected in this volume were all written (and for the most part published) during the period that spanned my adolescence and early adulthood. The earliest among them, "The Boutique," was published when I was fifteen, and most of the rest were written in a spate of collegiate creativity before I turned nineteen. They largely reflect an adolescent sensibility: with one or two exceptions their concerns, their assumptions, and their language all emerge from the consciousness of an urban Indian male in his late teens.

To put them all in perspective, perhaps a few general words of background are in order. I wrote from a very young age, my first "story" emerging when I was six. I was an asthmatic child, often bedridden with severe attacks, and rapidly exhausted the diversions available to me. I found few books on the family's shelves that appealed to me, and those I read inconveniently fast. Purchases were expensive and libraries limited: many libraries let you borrow only one book at a time, and I had an awkward tendency to finish that in the car on the way home. Perhaps the ultimate clincher was that there was no television in the Bombay of my boyhood. So I wrote.

My imagination overcame my wheezing. My first stories were imitative school mysteries like those by Enid Blyton that all my classmates read. By the time I was nine I was attempting to churn out heroic tales of wartime derring-do. Here I was more than derivative: I abandoned any patriotic pretensions and wrote about an RAF fighter pilot called Reginald Bellows. When the first installment of *Operation Bellows* appeared in a new youth magazine, I was a month short of my eleventh birthday.

There is nothing quite like the thrill of first seeing your writing in print. It ranks with the other great moments of your life, the first school prize, the first kiss, the first smile from your baby. I had found my *métier*.

My next few stories continued to be inspired by my childhood reading. I remember a Stephen Crane-type U.S. Civil War story (where the Yankee father ended up killing his Confederate son on the battleground, or it may have been the other way around) and one about a pair of school children who save a young king from assassination at his own coronation (the Shah's imperial extravaganza to mark the 2,500th year of his mythical dynasty was much in the news at the time, I believe). Finally, as I became a teenager, I started trying to depict the worlds I knew and saw around me. Improbable fantasies about distant lands seemed suddenly less interesting than writing about people like myself and the things that occupied our minds.

The audience was ready-made: Indians who read Indian mass-circulation magazines. I was writing to be published and read, not to pursue an obscure literary aesthetic. This in turn helped define the nature, and the limitations, of my work. In selecting these stories, I have omitted some that friends and family remember with pleasure but which now seem unworthy of resurrection. Yet the ones that have survived between these covers are fairly representative of the whole. I enjoyed writing them and hope some of that enjoyment proves communicable.

—S. T.

Acknowledgments

The stories in this collection originally appeared, some in slightly different form, in *JS*, *The Illustrated Weekly of India*, *Eve's Weekly*, *Youth Times*, *Gentleman*, *The New Review*, and *Cosmopolitan*. Today all but one of these journals is defunct, but I should like gratefully to recall them and thank the editors (or fiction editors) who encouraged my early writing—the late Desmond Doig, Gulshan Ewing, Sadhan (Charlie) Banerjee, Jug Suraiya, Dina Mehta and Anees Jung. They have all published many better stories than these, but by finding space for my work they launched me on an adventure in which I am still, these many years later, happily engaged.

In publishing this book I should also like to express my gratitude to many outside the magazine world whose advice and kindness I have never forgotten—Mrs. Gopi Gauba and Mrs. Tapati Mookerji, whose early praise for my fiction helped me acquire both confidence and discipline; the many school and college friends whose feedback was the source of my continuing inspiration; the late Erica Kalmer, agent and translator, who brought me to the attention of a European audience by publishing many of the stories in this collection in German; Sri Kesava in Singapore, a warm and engaging friend whose enthusiasm for these stories sadly coincided with economic misfortune; and Han Suyin, whose generous regard for my writing—and her exhortation that I must "engage in a long and pitiless novel, which will allow (my) talent a wider scope"—helped me persist at the keyboard. And a word of appreciation for the old (and new) friend who remembered many of these stories and who read this collection with wisdom and insight: thank you, Ramu.

The Five-Dollar Smile

AND OTHER STORIES

The Five-Dollar Smile

"MAKE THIS CHILD SMILE AGAIN," the black type on the crumpled, glossy news weekly page read. "All it takes is five dollars a month."

Joseph stared at the picture sandwiched between the two halves of the caption. He had seen it a thousand times—the tattered clothes, the dark, intense, pleading eyes, the grubby little fingers thrust tightly into a sullenly closed mouth. The photo that had launched the most successful, worldwide appeal in HELP's history, four years ago. His picture.

As usual, he viewed it once more with that curious detachment that had come to him during those last four years. He could not see it as a photograph of himself, a record of his past, a souvenir of his younger childhood. It was not personal enough for that; it was in the public domain, part of an advertisement, a poster, a campaign, and now an aging magazine clipping in his hand. The little boy who stared out at him was not him, Joseph Kumaran; he was part of a message, defined by a slogan, serving a purpose, and the fact that he was Joseph Kumaran did not matter. It never had.

Joseph looked once more at the picture, as he had five times already during the flight, as if to reassure himself that he knew what he was doing on this large, cold, humming monster hurtling him towards a strange land he had known only in postage stamps. That's what this is all about, he wanted the picture to say. That's who you are and the reason why you are on an unfamiliar thing called an airplane and why your feet don't touch the ground but your toes feel cold and you have to put a belt around your waist that stops you from leaning forward comfortably to eat the strange food they expect you to get at with plastic forks and knives, sealed impossibly in polyethylene, while you wish you could pluck up the nerve to ask the poised, distant, and impossibly tall, white lady to help you, help you with a blanket and two pillows and some real food you can eat without trying to gnaw at sealed packages of cutlery. . . .

He folded the picture again and pushed it into the pocket of the tight little blazer he had been given the day he left the HELP office with Sister Celine to go to the airport. It had been sent with a bundle of old clothes for the disaster relief collection, he had learned, and though it was a little small for him it was just the thing to smarten him up for the trip to the United States. "Always be smart, Joseph," Sister Celine had said. "Let them know you're poor but you're smart, because we knew how to bring you up."

Joseph sat back, his feet dangling from the airplane seat, and looked at the largely uneaten food on the tray. When he thought of food he could remember the day of the photograph. He had been seven then: that was the day he had learned he was seven.

"How old's that little kid? The one in the torn white shirt?"

"He's about seven. No one's really sure. He came here when he was a little child. We couldn't really tell when he'd been born."

"About seven, eh. Looks younger." *Click, whirr.* "Might be what I'm looking for. Get him away from that food, Sister, will you please? We want a hungry child, not a feeding one."

Suddenly, a large, white hand interposed among the tiny, out-stretched brown ones crowded at the table, pulling Joseph's away. "Come here, Joseph. This nice man wants to see you."

"But I want to eat, Sister." Desperation, pleading in his voice. He knew what could happen if he was too late. There would be no food left for him: it had happened before. And today was his favorite day, with crisp *papadams* in the *kanji* gruel. He had watched the cooks rip up and fry the *papadams* from behind the kitchen door, and he'd tried to get to the table early so he wouldn't miss out on his share. He'd had to fight the bigger boys to stay there, too. But what determined resistance had preserved, Sister Celine was taking away.

"Please, Sister, please."

"Later, child. Now behave yourself." He was dragging his feet and she was pulling him quite firmly by the left hand. "And if you don't walk properly I shall have to take the cane to you." He straightened up quickly; he knew the cane well and did not want it again.

Would the stewardess take a cane to him if he asked her for a fork and knife? Of course she wouldn't, he knew that. He knew his nervousness was silly, unnecessary. He was suddenly hungry, but he didn't know how to attract her attention. She was giving a man a drink several rows in front of Joseph.

"Miss!" he called softly. His voice came out huskily, tripping over dry obstacles in his throat. She didn't hear him; he wished desperately that she would catch his eye, and he trained his look on her with such fearful intensity it was unbelievable she should not notice. "Miss!" he called again, waving his hand. She was sticking a pin into the headrest of the man who'd bought the drink, and she still didn't hear.

"Miss!" This time it was too loud. It seemed to Joseph that everyone in the plane had turned to look at him, as if he had done something very odd. There were a couple of smiles, but for the most part people looked disapproving, frowning their displeasure at him and making comments to their neighbors. Joseph's dark cheeks flushed red with embarrassment.

The stewardess straightened up, controlled her irritation, and smiled sweetly but briskly as she walked down to him. "Yes, what is it?"

"Can-I-have-a-knife-and-fork-please?" The words came out in a rush, Sister Angela's diction lessons forgotten in his anxiety.

She hardly seemed to pause in her stride. "It's on your tray—here, on the side, see? In this packet." And she lifted the packet, placed it on top of the napkin for him to see, and before he could say anything more, strode off down the aisle.

"Hold it there, kid." Joseph, seven, wanting *papadams*, confronted American slang for the first time in the person of a large, white man with a mustache and a camera. To little Joseph, everything seemed large about the man: his body, his mustache, his camera. A large hand pushed him back a little and a voice boomed: "Seems rather small for his age."

"Infant malnutrition. Mother died in childbirth and his father brought him through the forest alone. These tribals are astonishingly hardy. God knows how he survived without any permanent damage."

"So there's nothing really wrong with him, right? I mean, his brain's okay and everything? I've gotta be sure I'm selling the American public poverty and not retardation, if you see what I mean. So he's normal, huh?"

"Just a little stunted." Sister Celine, quiet, precise. *Click, whirr.* Lights exploded at him. His eyes widened.

"Let's take him outside, if you don't mind. I'd like to use the sun—I'm not too sure of my flash."

"Yes, of course, Mr. Cleaver. Come, Joseph."

He squirmed out of the nun's grasp. "But, Sister, I want to eat."

"Later. Now if you're difficult there'll be no lunch at all for you."

Resentfully, he followed them out into the courtyard. He stood there sullenly, staring his quiet hatred at the large man. *Click, whirr, click.* "Move him to this side a bit, won't you, Sister?"

It was being pushed around that made him thrust his fingers into his mouth, as much in self-protection as in appeasement of his palate. The photographer clicked again.

Joseph turned to look at the stewardess' retreating back in profound dismay. Why hadn't he told her that he knew he had a knife and fork, but he didn't know how to get at them? Why hadn't he made clear what exactly was the help he needed? Why had he been so scared?

He drew himself even more deeply into his seat and looked around nervously. His neighbor, staring out the window, smiled briefly, mechanically, at him. Joseph could not ask him to help. Or could he? The man turned from the window to a magazine he was reading over dinner. Joseph's resolution faded.

That day, after the photographs, there had been no *papadams* left for him. Only cold *kanji;* the *papadams* were already finished.

"See—I told you you could have lunch later," the nun said. "Here's your lunch now."

But I wanted the *papadams*, he wanted to scream in rage and frustration. And why did you need to take me away from my *papadams?* What was so important about that man with the camera that you had to deprive me of something I've been waiting a month to enjoy? But he did not say all that. He could not. Instead, the lump in his throat almost choking him, he flung the tin plate of gruel to the ground and burst into tears.

"Good heavens—what's the matter with him today? Very well, no lunch for you then, Joseph. And you will clean this mess off the floor and come to my office as soon as you have done so, so that you may be suitably punished for your ingratitude. There are many little boys not as fortunate as you are, Joseph Kumaran. And don't you forget it."

Sniffing back his misery, Joseph knew he would not forget it. He would have six strokes of the cane to remember it by.

How could he ask his neighbor to help open the packet? He was so engrossed in his magazine. And he was eating. It seemed so wrong, and so embarrassing. Joseph tried to speak, but the words would not come out.

At the head of the aisle, another stewardess was already bringing tea or coffee around. The other passengers seemed to be finishing their meals. They would take his tray away from him and he would not even have eaten. A panic, irrational but intense, rose to flood him.

He struggled with the packet. He tried to tear it, gnaw at it, rip it open. It would not give way. The cutlery inside the packet jangled; at one point he hit a cup on his tray and nearly broke it. Joseph's attempts became even wilder and he made little noises of desperation.

"Here," his neighbor's strong voice said. "Let me help you."

Joseph turned to him in gratitude. He had hoped his desperation would become apparent and attract assistance. It had worked.

"Thank you," he managed to say. "I didn't know how to open it."

"It's quite easy," his neighbor said.

The first copies of the photographs arrived at the HELP Center a few weeks after the photographer had left. Joseph had almost forgotten the incident, even the caning, though the frustration of the *papadam*-less gruel remained. One of the nuns called him to Sister Eva's office excitedly.

"Look, Joseph—these are the pictures the nice man took, the day you were so bad," Sister Celine told him. "This is you."

Joseph looked at the black-and-white image without curiosity. He would rather not have seen it, rather not have been reminded of their perverse cruelty to him that day. He stared at the picture, made no comment, and looked away.

"It's going to be used in a worldwide appeal," Sister said. "Your picture will be in every important magazine in the world. Helping us get money to help other children. Doesn't that make you happy, Joseph?"

He had learned to be dutiful. "Yes, Sister," he said.

The man in the seat next to him turned the polyethylene packet around, slipped out a flap, and deftly extricated a fork and a knife. He handed them to Joseph with a cordial smile.

"There—you see, easy."

"Thank you." Joseph, taking the implements from the man, felt his ears burning with shame. So there had been no need to try and tear open the packet after all. There was a flap. He turned single-mindedly to the food, wanting to shut the rest of the world, witness to his humiliation, out of his sight and hearing.

The first MAKE THIS CHILD SMILE AGAIN poster was put up in the HELP office just behind Sister Eva's desk, so those who came in would be struck by it as soon as they entered and looked for her. It was put up without any fuss or ceremony, and Joseph only knew it was there because the door to Sister Eva's office had been open when he and a group of boys had been walking down the corridor to their daily classes. It was one of the other boys who had noticed it first and drawn everyone else's attention to it.

The slogan soon became a joke. "Smile, Joseph, smile," his friends would tease him. And if he was in a particularly angry mood, one of the boys would ask with mock gravity, "Has anyone got five dollars?" Sometimes Joseph would only get angrier, but sometimes he would be provoked to smile at them. They used to call it the five-dollar smile.

The food was terrible. It was totally unfamiliar to Joseph's taste buds, anyway, and he did not enjoy it. There was, however, a bowl of fruit salad on the tray that contained little diced apples. He ate those, spilling some on the seat and the floor. He did not know whether to be happy about the pieces he had eaten or sad about the ones he had lost. He looked around to see if anyone was watching him. No one was. He tried to pick up a little piece of apple from the floor, but the tray was in his way and he couldn't reach down far enough. It was frustrating. On balance, he felt miserable.

The stewardess swished by to collect his tray. Would he like some tea? Joseph said, "Yes." Actually he wanted coffee, but he was scared that if he said "no" to the tea he might not be offered any coffee either. Why couldn't they have offered him coffee first? he thought, as the pale, brown liquid filled his cup. It was so unfair.

He was, not surprisingly, the first child to be "adopted." Other people who responded to the campaign had sent in their five dollars for the first month, and their pledges for a year or two years or a decade or a lifetime, for any child HELP wanted to rescue. But three couples insisted their money go to one specific child—the child in the photograph. They had seen his sad, little face, and they wanted to make him smile again. No one else. Their five dollars were for Joseph Kumaran's tiny little fingers to come out of his hungry little mouth. And they insisted on being allowed to adopt him alone.

The nuns had sighed when those letters came in. "Oh, what a nuisance some people are," Sister Eva said. "I have half a mind to return their money to them. It's none of their business to tell us where their money should go." But Sister Eva had kept the money and the pledges anyway—from all three couples. Joseph Kumaran's five-dollar smile was actually netting HELP fifteen dollars a month.

So every month Joseph would have to sit down and, in his neat, strained little hand, write a letter to each of his foster parents, thousands of miles away, telling them how good and grateful he was. "Today we had catechism, and I learned the story of how Lot's wife turned into a banana tree," he would write to one couple. (Salt was an expensive commodity in those parts, and the nuns didn't want the children to derive the wrong lessons from the Bible.) Then he would copy the same line out neatly onto the other two letters. As he grew older, Sister Celine would no longer dictate the letters, but let him write them himself and correct them before they were mailed. "Sister Angela has told me about America," he wrote once. "Is it true that everyone is rich there and always has plenty to eat?" Sister Celine did not like that, scored it out, and was later seen speaking sternly to Sister Angela.

The steward was coming down the aisle selling headphones. Joseph had seen him doing that as the flight began, and though he did not know what headphones were, he had discovered that they cost money and that people put them into their ears. He shook his head vigorously when asked whether he wanted one. But his anxious eyes rolled in curiosity as his neighbor, who had also declined the first time, looked at the movie handbill in approbation, produced green notes and silver coins, and was rewarded with a polyethylene packet. From this emerged a contraption even stranger at close quarters than it had seemed from a distance.

The curtains were being drawn across the airplane windows; a screen was lowered at the head of the cabin; images flickered on the whiteness ahead. Joseph stared, transfixed, rapt. His neighbor had plugged in his headset and was obviously listening to something Joseph could not hear. Titles began to appear on the screen.

Joseph desperately wanted to hear the movie, too.

He would get letters in reply from his foster parents. Initially, they were as frequent as his monthly letters to them, but later their interest seemed to flag and he would get only occasional replies. One couple seemed the nicest—they would always apologize profusely whenever their letters were too late, and they would always ask about him, his schoolwork, his games. At Christmas they would send little gifts that Sister Celine would let him open but which he would have to share with the other children. Joseph liked their colored notepaper, the lady's handwriting, which was so easy to read, and the lingering smell of perfume that still clung to each sheet of stationery. Frequently he would hold it up to his face, smothering his nose in it, smelling America.

One day, after several letters to this couple, he became bolder. "It is very hot here at this time of year," he had written in the version approved by Sister Celine "I suppose it is cooler in America." But while copying the corrected draft out neatly on to an aerogram, he added: "I think I would enjoy America very much." He told no one about the addition, sealed the aerogram, and waited excitedly for a reply.

When it came, there was no reference to what he had written. But Joseph did not give up. "I often wonder whether America has trees like the ones in my drawing," he hinted while enclosing a precocious crayon sketch. And in the next letter, "If I came to America, do you think I might like it?" He was so enamored of this approach that he copied that line into each of his three letters and sent them away.

It worked. His favorite "parents," the ones who sent him Christmas presents, wrote to Sister Celine to say that they'd often wanted to see the little boy they'd "adopted" but they'd never been able to manage a trip to India. Would it not be possible for young Joseph to be sent to America instead? As soon as they heard from Sister Celine, they would be happy to enclose a plane ticket for the little boy. Of course, they were not suggesting that he should stay with them always. Obviously, his place was among "his people" in India, and "with you all at HELP." They would send him back, but they did so want to see him, just once.

Sister Celine seemed a little taken aback by the letter. It was not customary for foster parents to evince such an interest in their protégés. When they were old enough the children were simply taught an elementary trade and packed off to earn their keep. Foreign trips, for however short a duration, were highly unusual.

Sister Celine showed Joseph the letter and asked, "You haven't been up to anything, have you?" To his excited protestations she merely responded, "We'll see." And then she went to talk to Sister Eva.

Joseph had only seen one movie before. That was a documentary about HELP's activities among orphan children in the wilds of Bihar, and it had been shown one evening after dinner by the man who made it, so that the nuns could all see what the outside world was being told about their work. Sister Eva, in a spirit of generosity, had suggested that the boys, at least those over five, be permitted to sit on the ground and watch it too. It might teach them a few things, she told the other nuns, make them realize how much we do for them, maybe instill some gratitude in them. Joseph had fallen asleep halfway through that movie. He didn't want to see starving Adivasi children and warm-hearted nuns; he saw them every day. The black-and-white images, the monotonous, superimposed voice of the commentator, blurred in his mind; the nuns danced tiptoe through the crevices of his brain, and the pictures pulsed and faded in his eyes. Firm but gentle hands were rousing him.

"Get up—it's time to go to bed."

In the background, Sister Eva's high-pitched voice rang through the clear night: "Look at them! Give them a special treat like this and half of them go off to sleep! Don't ever let me catch any of you asking to see a movie again. I mean it!"

But what a movie this was. Bright, vivid colors, pretty, white women in short dresses, fast cars racing down broad, foreign streets. It was like nothing he had ever seen before. And he wanted to hear it; hear the loud roar of the car engines, the soft, tinkling laughter of the women, the shouts and the screams and all the sounds of bullets and people and whizzing airplanes.

"Sir." The steward who had dispensed the headphones was standing at the end of the aisle, just behind Joseph, watching the movie too.

"Yes?"

"May I have some headphones too?"

"Of course." The steward disappeared behind the partition and emerged with a polyethylene packet. He handed it to Joseph.

Joseph reached out to take it with an ineffable feeling of awe, wonder, and achievement. He pushed aside the flap, put in his hand, and touched the cold plastic. The sensation was indescribably thrilling.

"Two dollars and fifty cents, please."

"But . . . but . . . I don't have any money," Joseph said miserably. His eyes pleaded with the steward. "Please?"

The steward had a why-are-you-wasting-my-time-you-dumb-child look on his face. "I'm sorry," he said, taking the packet out of Joseph's hands, "IATA regulations."

And then he was gone, having invoked an authority higher than Joseph's longings, more powerful than philanthropy. When he reemerged from the partition it was on the other side, on the aisle away from Joseph's.

Sister Eva had taken some time to decide. It was not that she minded in principle, she told Sister Celine, but this could set a dangerous precedent. The other children would be wanting to go too, and how many had rich American foster parents who would be willing to mail them plane tickets?

In the end, however, to Joseph's great relief, she agreed. She would write personally to the American couple making it clear Joseph was not to be spoiled. And that he was to be back within a month, before he could become entirely corrupted by American ways, to resume his place among those as unfortunate as he was. Unless they wanted to keep him in America for good, which they showed no intention of doing.

The next few weeks passed in a frenzy of preparation. The ticket had to arrive, a flight had to be booked, a passport had to be issued to Joseph, a visa obtained. He was given a little suitcase for his clothes, and he swelled with pride at his tangible evidence of possessions. He had things, he was somebody. With a passport, a suitcase, a ticket, he was not just a little brown face in a crowd around the gruel bowl; he was Master Joseph Kumaran, and he was going somewhere.

And finally, wearing the tight blazer he had been given on the morning of his departure, its pocket stuffed with the newsmagazine clipping he had hoarded since it had been shown to him by Sister Celine four years ago, his passport nestling next to a glossy color photo of his hosts sent to him so that he would recognize them at the airport, Joseph was put on board the plane. Sister Celine was there to see him off; she smiled at him through misty glasses, and Joseph felt the wetness on her cheeks when she hugged him at the departure gate. But he could not cry in return; he was a little scared, but more excited than upset, and he certainly was not sad.

The man sitting next to him did not seem to care particularly for the movie after all. Twice, Joseph caught him dozing off, his eyes closing and his chin sinking slowly to his chest; twice, with equal suddenness, his neighbor's head would jerk awake, prompted no doubt by some startling sound on the headphones. The third time this happened, the man pulled off his headphones in disgust and strode off, clambering over Joseph, in quest of a sink.

Joseph could not resist this opportunity. It was too good to be true: headphones plugged in, next to him, unused. He eased himself out of his seatbelt and sat in his neighbor's chair. Then, tentatively, looking around him to make sure no one had noticed him, he raised the tips to his ears. Almost immediately he was assaulted by the sounds of the movie: brakes screeched as a car drew to a halt; a man dashed down some stairs with a gun in his hand; there was some panting dialogue; the gun went off, the bullet's report a deafening symphony in Joseph's ear; a woman screamed. And his neighbor returned from the toilet.

Joseph looked up, almost in agony. His pleasure had been so brief.

The man smiled down at him from the aisle. "Mine, sonny," he beamed.

Joseph had been well brought up. "Excuse me," he said, gently removing the headphones and placing them on the seat. He slid into his place again, his neighbor returned to his chair, the earplugs went back on, and Joseph found he could not see the screen through his tears.

Hoping his neighbor would not notice, he dabbed at his eyes with the clean, white handkerchief Sister Angela had pressed into his hand that morning. That morning—it seemed so long ago. He returned the handkerchief to his pocket, feeling once again the magazine clipping that, four years ago, had started him on this journey. Resolutely, he refrained from pulling it out. That was not him: he had another identity now. He took out his passport, and his eyes caressed each detail on the inside page, from the fictional birthdate ("it's easier than going through the entire 'birthdate unknown' business," Sister Eva had declared) to the inventory of his characteristics ("Hair: black; eyes: black; skin: brown") to the new, awkward photograph, Joseph staring glassy-eyed into the studio camera. And then, returning the passport at long last to his inside pocket, he touched the other photo, the glossy, color portrait of his new, albeit temporary, parents. After some hesitation, he took it out: these were the people whose house he would call home for the next month.

But would he really? He stared at their forms in the photograph. They had sent Joseph their picture so he would recognize them, but they had not asked for his. "We're sure we'll spot him as soon as he gets off the plane," the wife had written to Sister Celine. "We feel we've known him all our lives." Joseph had felt flattered then, deeply touched. Then one day, in a fit of temper, Sister Eva had threatened to replace Joseph with another little dark-skinned boy from the orphanage. "Do you think they'd be able to tell the difference?" she had demanded.

In silent, desperate misery, Joseph had not known what to say.

Looking at the photograph, Joseph tried to think of the magic of America, of things there he had heard about and dreamed of—

movies, parties, delicious food of infinite variety, outings to the beach and to Disneyland. But his eyes dilated and the photograph blurred. He did not know why he felt suffused with a loneliness more intense, more bewildering in its sadness than he had ever experienced in the gruel crowds of HELP. He was alone, lost somewhere between a crumpled magazine clipping and the glossy brightness of a color photograph.

On the seat next to him, his neighbor snored peacefully, chin resting in surrender on his chest, headphones embedded into his ears. On the screen, the magic images flickered, cascaded, and danced on.

1978

The Boutique

The elevator attendant swung open the door of the elevator and looked at Amma and me with an appraisingly critical eye.

From his manner it was clear he wasn't very impressed: Amma in her plain cotton sari with her slightly greying hair done up in a traditional way at the back, clutching the invitation card as if for security and looking very plain and rather proletarian; me in my loose *kurta* that fell awkwardly from bony shoulders, in narrow trousers that went out of fashion five years back, sporting an unshaven underchin, looking more unkempt than dashing.

He elevated an eyebrow ever so slightly and moved infinitesimally to the left, as though making way for appearance's sake. I waved Amma into the elevator as she stepped in awkwardly, unsure of herself, and followed, trying to look confident and extroverted. The attendant didn't move; he waited for further passengers—there was no one in sight—while we fidgeted uneasily, then turned his face a fraction towards me. "Where to?" he asked.

"The new boutique opening," Amma answered for me, trying

to assert herself. "In the . . . er . . ."—she looked at the card—
"Plaza Lounge. Which floor is that?"

The attendant looked at her incredulously, then contemptu-
ously. He nodded in sage understanding and made to shut the
elevator door. In the distant entrance to the hotel foyer, a fat lady
in a dress of some expensive material waddled through and the
attendant paused in his act for her to make her way to the elevator.
He could have left us at the first floor and come back for her in that
time; but he waited, and so did we. I suddenly felt like rushing out
of the elevator, the hotel, the area. This wasn't our place. We
didn't belong here.

But I didn't. Poor Amma had been so desperately keen on
coming to attend the new boutique opening, and despite my
reluctance I had agreed to escort her. Father had a minor desk
job in the editorial department of the city's leading paper, and he
often got these invitations. He always brought them home
proudly as if to show to Amma and me he wasn't as much of
a failure as we knew he was, and they lay on the solitary bedroom table as cardboard symbols of his prestige. We rarely used
them.

But this was one time Amma was insistent. She had always
been anxious to see how the mod sophisticates she had heard
about lived; now here was an opportunity to see them in their
natural habitat. She couldn't throw away this chance of a lifetime,
and she couldn't go alone. So she dragged me along.

The fat lady reached the elevator, and the attendant stepped
aside in deference to let her in. She was about Amma's age, I
guessed; she wore a wig, an excess of makeup, a lot of real-looking
jewelry and an air of haughty superiority. A reek of some expensive perfume preceded her by a good ten yards. Amma stepped
back uncomfortably into the darkest recesses of the elevator as she
entered.

The door shut and the elevator proceeded smoothly upwards. I
saw Amma trying not to look at the fat lady, and I felt a wave of

pity and compassion surge up in me. Instinctively, I put a hand on her arm. Don't worry, Amma, I thought, I'll protect you. "Protect you?" the words mocked me in my mind. "From what?" I hastily dropped my hand from her arm.

The elevator stopped, the door opened, and the fat lady stepped out first. It was natural, unquestioned; it was her due. I let Amma follow and then stepped out too, with a "thank you" to the attendant. He ignored me completely.

Amma was overawed by the landing leading to the suite where the boutique was; the wall-to-wall carpeting, the air-conditioned atmosphere, the little groups of suited-and-booted people. Suddenly I too felt out of my class. I started wishing I had paid more attention to my appearance. I looked into one of the mirrored columns and hastily, furtively, smoothed back my hair.

People were walking into the boutique now. There were not very many of them; perhaps fifteen, perhaps twenty. We were late; the speeches and ribbon-cutting, if there had been any, appeared to be over. People were standing around in twos and threes, sipping coffee served by a uniformed waiter and examining some of the objects for sale. Amma and I hesitantly went in. No one took any notice of us whatsoever.

The waiter passed us, looking through us without pausing in his stride. I thought at first that the coffee had to be paid for, then saw him offering steaming hot cups of it to all the visitors. Anyone who chose to could take a cup of coffee. I felt a wave of anger rising up in me. We had been insulted.

I halted him as he turned back with a half-empty tray by physically standing in his path. "Here too," I said. He glowered at me resentfully for a second, then proffered the tray to me. I took a cup and waved him on to Amma. Reluctantly he complied. Amma refused him with a thank you and a smile.

"Why did you do that, Amma?" I asked after the waiter had moved away. "I thought you liked coffee." She didn't reply; instead she looked around her and said, "Come, let's see what there is here." I followed her to the tastefully decorated section for men's garments.

There were a few people looking at the clothes put up for sale. A young couple hovered around indecisively, and a smiling sales-girl came up to them and asked, "Can I help you?" They said "No, thanks," and she went away. She saw us, equally uncertain, but ignored us all the same.

Amma looked at the impressive array of shirts, ties and jackets before her. One jacket, in black leather, especially attracted her. "I've always wanted you to have something like this, son," she said, "and God knows we haven't been able to afford to buy you anything. But looking at you in your plain clothes, and seeing these boys here in such fine attire—I want you to have this. I know it will suit you, my son. You are a handsome boy, and this will look good on you." She fingered the sleeve. There was no price tag attached. Poor Amma was captivated by it. I wanted to say no, Amma, I don't want it, I don't need it at all, I am quite content with the clothes I have, but I could imagine myself in that leather jacket, the envy of the boys and the wonder of the girls in the neighborhood, and no words came out of my lips. I watched her, half in hope and half in anticipation.

Amma caressed the jacket, and took it off its hanger. "Come closer, my son," she said, placing it against my body so she could see me with it. "It looks wonderful. I wonder how much it will cost."

"Here, you can't touch the articles," the salesgirl said, coming up behind Amma suddenly. "Can't you see the sign?" she pointed to a PLEASE DON'T TOUCH card among the clothes. "Don't you know English?"

Amma flushed a deep red. "I'm sorry," she mumbled in confu-sion, hastily trying to put it back. "I was just . . . I didn't see . . . how much does it cost?"

The salesgirl took the jacket from her hands and looked at her pityingly. "Seven hundred rupees," she said.

Amma was completely thrown off her guard by the entirely unexpected figure. "What . . . pardon me . . . seven hundred rupees?" She asked in confused embarrassment.

"That's right, ma'am," the girl said, placing the jacket back in its place. "And please don't touch the clothes."

"It's all right, Amma," I said. "I didn't want it anyway. What shall I do with a jacket like this?" Amma still looked miserable, so I added, "Anyway it's far too big for me—I'd look like a scarecrow in a wrestler's leftovers if I wore this." She wasn't consoled.

Just then a famous radio disc jockey entered the boutique, and all eyes turned in his direction. Tall and ruggedly handsome, he wore a silk shirt and scarf and flared trousers, and I envied him like hell. He strode to the men's clothing salesgirl and said, "Hi."

"Oh, hello, Jay," the girl said, "we've got something you'll really like—the newest thing in ties, and *so* inexpensive. Isn't this one fabulous? And it's *just* seventy."

"Hmm," the deejay said in casual approbation, flipping through the ties on the rack. Somehow I couldn't take my eyes off him. He was everything I wanted to be, impressive, polished, well-dressed, popular—and rich. Amma was looking at him too, sorting the ties out, liking one color here, objecting to another's width there, and all the while her eyes were traveling from his hands to the PLEASE DON'T TOUCH card nestling unnoticed among the little heap of sartorial rejects at the bottom of the rack. Suddenly I felt physically sick; I wanted to get out of there, get out of the rarefied, air-conditioned atmosphere, off the wall-to-wall carpeted floor, away from the mirrors on every column that thrust reminders at me of what I really was. A kind of nausea overtook me, and momentarily my head swam, converting the floor, the walls, the mirrors, the designs and patterns and decorations and clothes, into a whirling, twisting question mark, asking me, "What are you doing here?" And suddenly I realized I didn't know, I didn't know what I was doing there, and the question mark straightened itself out in my mind to an arrow, a line, and I knew where the line led—outside, to the relief of the hot pavement and the elegiac gloom of the evening shut out by the brocaded, mirrored walls of the Plaza Lounge.

"Amma," I said, clutching her sleeve. "Let's go."

But she didn't seem to be listening. There was a strange, semi-determined, half-surprised look on her face, and she was moving away from me. I recognized that look; I had often seen it when I had done something wrong at home and she had turned on me breathing "ingrate." Suddenly I realized what she was going to do. I tried to stop her but she had already reached the counter.

"Here," she was saying in a loud, shrill voice of complaint, "I thought we weren't supposed to touch the clothes."

An offended silence descended upon the congregation. Faces turned to look at us. Amma looked up, a trifle defiantly, expecting an apology or a reprimand but prepared for either, at the salesgirl. The deejay, too, turned from his flirtation with the ties and the women and gave us the benefit of a mildly offended look. Then he turned back and resumed his conversation with the salesgirl. The hubbub of voices around us resumed. The pause was over; our clumsy intrusion had largely been forgotten. But in the harder lines of the salesgirl's face I knew it would never be forgiven.

"Amma—let's go." She stood still for a moment, incredulity and hurt writ all over her face, and then slowly, resignedly, without a trace of bitterness or resentment, subsided and walked away from the counter. When she spoke there was a break in her voice.

"Yes, son—let's . . . go."

Quietly, sadly, we walked to the door. No one noticed our exit; it was as if an insect had been removed from a cup of tea, something which ought not to have been there in the first place had been ejected. I evaded the eyes of a passing bearer.

We used the stairs. When we walked out of the hotel and on to the street the ambience was oppressive. I wanted to pick up a brick, a stone, a tile from the pavement, anything, and throw it at the glass front of the building. But I didn't. I couldn't, I didn't have the right to.

"Let's take a taxi, son," Amma said.

"No, Amma," I replied and suddenly the lump in my throat wasn't that big any more. "We'll walk to the bus stop. As usual."

Something in my tone made her turn and look up at me.

I smiled. "We're going home, Amma," I said.

I felt the pressure of her hand on my arm as we walked slowly on to join the line waiting for the bus.

1971

How Bobby Chatterjee Turned to Drink

As soon as I walked into the barroom of the Saturday Club I knew something was wrong.

The Light Horse Bar isn't normally one of those places where one collapses heavily onto the bar stool and asks the willing Boniface to come up with his strongest. It belongs rather to the quiet, plush variety of cocktail lounges where one threads a business acquaintance through one's own commercial needle via a few glasses of the needful and then thinks of the bill later. Public displays of emotion, therefore, are as rare as modest copywriters, if not rarer, and the day when Jimmy Khandelwala fell over the precipice of sobriety and smashed a wine goblet back in 1952 is still spoken of with tearful nostalgia by old habitués.

Today, however, it was easily apparent that the same old h's would have something more recent to wax eloquent about. For seated on the only occupied bar stool on the premises, tie in disarray, hair looking like something out of a "before Brylcreem" ad, staring with fixed concentration at a half full glass of purest Scotch, and emitting at irregular intervals little growls of varying intensity which increased in volume and depth whenever any solicitous fellow-inmate happened to pass within hand-shaking range, was Bobby Chatterjee, looking like a man who had just seen his mother-in-law's reincarnation. Now if I tell you that Bobby never touched the stuff in normal circumstances and considered liquor the cause of All the Ills of Our Society, you'll understand my surprise. Dash it, I was more than surprised; I felt as shocked as a clumsy electrician. Seeking like an American GI in Vietnam for the light at the end of the tunnel, I ambulated on uncertain feet to where two of the ad agency crowd sat, looking grim.

"I say . . . ," I began.

"Say no more," Jit stopped me with raised palm. "I know what you're thinking about. In fact, we're as surprised as you are." He nodded meaningfully in the general direction of Bobby's bar stool.

"You can say that again," added Ram morosely. "When I walked in, you could have knocked me over with a G-string."

I gave him an expressive look, but it bounced off him like a stone off a politician's car. I mean, I don't blame him. This was no time for expressive looks. Dammit, this thing was serious.

"Doesn't anybody know the reason for . . . this?" I queried, hesitating almost prophylactically before that last word.

"I do," said Cedric, emerging from behind us like a villain in the third act of a Victorian drama, "and if you chaps will stand me a John Collins, rally around and I'll tell you the tale."

Establishing consensus with the speed of a Warsaw Pact conference on freedom of speech, we acquiesced in relief and ushered him to a seat. After all, a John Collins was a small price to pay for a true exposé of the present situation. And Cedric is one of those fellows who knows everything; he always seems to have access to more privileged information than the resident CIA agent.

"Well, what's it all about?" Jit asked, hardly able to restrain himself.

"Waiter," Cedric signaled a passing admiral.

"Oh—a John Collins, please, waiter," I said.

"Sir." He vanished into the wilderness of bottles.

"Well?" Ram asked.

"Ah, Bobby," Cedric said, pausing while the waiter placed his drink before him, and taking a deep sip while I signed the chit. "You may have noticed, gentlemen, that our usually immaculate friend, Bobby Chatterjee Esq. of It's An Ad Ad Ad Ad World, Inc., if not exactly disheveled, is looking far from sheveled, to cut a fine phrase, as of this moment. He is also partaking rather generously of alcoholic liquor, the one vice—or so he had assiduously maintained—that he had not yet succumbed to. There is something about. . . ."

"Oh, cut the sales talk and come to the point," said Ram, who is only an Account Executive.

Cedric glared at him but saw unanimity of opinion ranged soundly behind the philistine. "Oh, well," he said, "if you insist. The reason for all—er—all this—is the universal one: the one cause of all the world's ills, etc., in short, love. Love came to poor Bobby Chatterjee's heart and broke it too." Here he paused for a long sip while the three of us exchanged incredulous glances.

"Bobby in love? But why, the fellow's a confirmed misogynist!" Jit exclaimed.

"*Was*, and *will be*," Cedric corrected, "but not *is*. Of course, there can be no doubt that the object of our discourse is at the present moment harboring dark thoughts about women in general and one member of the fair sex in particular, and then self-pity will give way to misogyny once more, but there is no altering the fact that love melted his hard, sales-oriented heart for once, and brought with it failure, disappointment, and drink (in that order) in its wake." Here he paused for breath and another gulp.

"But a charming, well-endowed, well-mannered adman like Bobby *falling* in love?" asked Ram, disbelieving. "Go on—tell that to the Marines."

"I would, if they'd stand me a *chota* peg," rejoined Cedric as he downed the rest of his drink and called for another. "This tale's enough to take any man down a *chota* peg or two."

We didn't laugh.

Bobby met Myra (Cedric said, sipping his second drink reflectively) at the ad agency studios, where she was to appear in one of their shorts—I mean film shorts, not the Jockey type. She was a fairly popular model, you must have seen her in those "Sex and the Single Shirt" ads, and there was an almost philanthropic generousness about her curves. Her figure, in short, would have met even an accountant's ideal. Account—figure, see? Heh-heh. (Here Cedric took another sip.)

Well, it was a case of Love At First Sight, and, as it normally is with confirmed misogynists, Bobby soon became convinced that Myra was the only girl in the world. He would worship the very ground she trod on, at least when it was carpeted, and he showered her with contracts to appear in ads for everything from cough drops to laxatives. As a result of all this, as you can easily understand, they were brought together pretty often, and what is called a close friendship soon began to develop. At these meetings Bobby missed no opportunity to show her how much he loved her, and he was soon delighted to find her more than responsive to his scarcely veiled advances. In fact, so Bobby told me, she even winked at him once, which sent him into raptures of sublime ecstasy.

The culmination of the affair (Cedric said hastily, as Jit glanced at his watch) came in the shape of a verbal invitation, delivered from "her own dear sweet lips" as Bobby put it, to spend the forthcoming weekend at her suburban Budge Budge home. Her father, now away on tour, was some kind of a big shot in a jute mill, and his sprawling bungalow nestling verdantly among garden foliage on the banks of the Hooghly was all hers for the moment. She had no mother. (On this happy note Cedric called for a third John Collins.)

From what she had told him, Bobby tells me (Cedric said) he got the idea of a pleasant and a romantic weekend in suburban solitude with only Myra for company. This idyllic picture was not, however, destined to outlast his arrival at Myra's place, smartly suited-and-booted in the nattiest of Burlington creations and looking like someone out of a Marlboro ad. Sophisticated, that's the word I'm groping for. He looked the charming, scintillating sophisticate that he was. And felt it.

Till Ali opened the door.

Bobby tells me he has never had a worse shock. He claims he nearly fell off the doorstep. For the bloke who opened the door was a bronzed, T-shirted-and-jeaned fellow with one of the fiercest mustaches Bobby had ever seen outside the motion pictures. It was black and curved and acquired new dimensions each time Bobby looked at it. And in addition to it all, the bloke was superbly fit and—what's the word?—lithe, that's it, lithe as a panther. One got a distinct impression of graceful ferocity, Bobby tells me. It was with a sinking feeling in the pit of his stomach that he answered the other's cheery good morning and entered the house.

For there could be no doubt about the fact that the mustachioed chap was a rival. Myra had assured him she'd have no relative around.

Whatever slight vestige of hope that was left—for hope, as the poet Burns, or was it Kutts, always used to say, springs eternal in the human breast—was shattered by Myra herself, entering the sitting room in a dazzling creation of red-and-green with flowers all over it. Bobby wasn't very descriptive or even very vivid, but he did say it had a neckline so low and a hemline so high that it was difficult to make out where the one began and the other ended. Anyway, it was a come-come costume to match her go-go earrings, but poor Bobby was not able to drink in the pleasures of the sight to the hilt. For in dulcet, voice-over tones she introduced him to the door-opener.

"Bobby, dear," Myra said, "this is Flight Lieutenant Rahim Ali, of the IAF. He's my other guest for the weekend." This, Bobby says, was accompanied by her most charming of smiles, but in his present frame of mind, he wasn't even able to appreciate that without wondering whether it was directed at him or at his aviator rival. To think that of all the things the fellow could have been— an unemployed engineer (there were a million of them), an Opposition politician or a long-distance runner with athlete's foot—he had to be an air force man. Musing bitterly over his fate, Bobby gave a sickly grin and handed over the box of chocolates he had hoped he and Myra would nibble over the Sunday. And she spoiled it all by offering Ali the first piece, which the blighter accepted with the most cocksure of thank-yous Bobby has ever heard, or so he says. It was distinctly revolting.

"Rahim, dear," Myra said, "do show Bobby where he can leave his things."

"Sure, Myra," Ali replied, still savoring his chocolate. "Follow me," he added to Bobby, as though addressing one of his bally mechanics, and strode with a familiar step to the stairs. As Bobby followed, Myra gave him a smile, which to his unappreciative eye seemed devoid of all the sweetness and light that had characterized it earlier. He returned a weaker grin than before and followed the rapidly ascending Ali posterior up the stairs.

Ali waved him to his room, waited for him to dump his stuff on the bed, and then said in a confidential undertone: "And if I were you, I'd take off all that effeminate stuff you're wearing. What are you—a man or a fop?" And without waiting for a reply from the speechless Bobby, he strode off with a jaunty step.

As Bobby descended the stairs to join Ali and Myra, he tells me, he was feeling as insecure as a nude at a stag party. That Ali was no mean rival, he was well aware. The blasted pilot was the biggest obstacle on his romantic path, but despite all the fellow's advantages Bobby was determined to overcome. He had come, he had seen; he'd be damned if he'd go away having conked out.

Thus braced for an uphill struggle, and consoling himself with the thought that surely a sweet girl like Myra would prefer a polite, well-mannered bloke (him) to an uncouth ruffian of Ali's genre, Bobby descended the stairs with a brave, if heavy, heart.

And then he stopped with a jolt. (Here Cedric called for his fourth and sipped it a little ruminatively before proceeding.)

The reason for Bobby's abrupt halt (Cedric said) was the fact that he had heard something, in Myra's voice, emanating from the sitting room, which took him aback rather. He had barely begun to believe his ears when he heard it again.

"Darling,"—it was unmistakably Myra—"I so admire strong men like you. You're so—so . . . *masculine*, darling; not like some *other* men I know."

To Bobby, in the light of what Ali had just advised him, the sentence seemed fraught with innuendo. Who else could the last part refer to but him? Broken, he stumbled back up the stairs. It was not until he had sat heavily on his bed that he began to ponder on his next course of action.

There was a stage in his thinking, Bobby tells me, when he even contemplated saying that he had just received an urgent telegram calling him back to town, or that he had forgotten something terribly important back in Calcutta that would necessitate a speedy return.

But the thought of Myra gave him renewed strength. This is not the stuff admen are made of, he told himself. Casting aside his pusillanimity and his woven-silk tie, he arose from his bed, fresh and determined. He would change his colors, too; don faded jeans with a patch in an awkward spot, pull on a bedraggled T-shirt and speak out of the corner of his mouth like Humphrey Bogart, not forgetting to drawl like John Wayne or smile enigmatically like Marlon Brando. That would bring him back into the he-man sweepstakes with a vengeance.

If he had only paused at the foot of the stairs before stumbling his way back up (Cedric said), Bobby would have been spared the agony of un-natting himself from his treasured Burlington suit-and-tie. For Myra—and I have this from her, myself—had only been rehearsing her lines in her next commercial, saying them aloud while Ali had gone to the WC so as to fix them in her memory. The dialogue, she told me when I rushed to her for an explanation, had run something like this:

FEMALE MODEL: "Darling, I so admire strong men like you. You're so—so . . . *masculine*, darling; not like some *other* men I know."

MALE MODEL: "It's nice of you to say so, my sweet. And I owe it all to Horlicks."

You know the type. And think—if Bobby had walked in, he'd have found Myra repeating the very same lines aloud to the empty air, and she'd have explained the whole thing to him and he'd have dismissed his fears with a laugh. But instead, Bobby stumbled up the stairs, a broken, dejected man. That's Fate.

When Bobby reached the sitting room in his new attire Ali had returned—not that Bobby had known that he'd ever been gone, of course. The cool pilot surveyed Bobby as though he were a defective altimeter or something and then remarked, "So I see you've changed."

"Bobby, dear, why did you get rid of those perfectly charming clothes?" Myra asked, and her tone, to Bobby, seemed bloody sarcastic, and he winced. He was not to know, of course, that Myra much preferred his style of dressing to Ali's. His change had been on the basis of her overheard utterance, and that, as the tragedy kings of print always say, was his undoing.

"Aw, thought I'd change into something more pleasant," Bobby said, out of the corner of his mouth.

"Beg your pardon, Bobby?"

"I thought I'd change into something more pleasant," Bobby repeated, finding some difficulty in lateral articulation.

"Poor Bobby—do you have a blister in your mouth, dear? I just can't seem to understand what you're saying."

"I thought I'd change into something more pleasant," Bobby yelled, his tongue getting almost inextricably tangled up with his molars, causing him to utter an involuntary "ouch" towards the end of his sentence.

"Oh dear, it is bad," Myra clucked sympathetically. "Rahim, do you think you have something for a blister?"

"I do not have a blister, Myra," Bobby said, trying to keep his voice down while drawling in the manner of John W. He had given up the Humphrey bogey.

"Then whatever's the matter with your articulation?" Myra asked irritably. "You used to be able to speak sentences in the past without sounding like a hydrophobic canine with throat cancer."

What made it worse, Bobby tells me, was the sight of the bloodhound Ali, sitting back and enjoying his discomfiture. It raised his hackles, causing him to commit excesses which under more normal circumstances he would have shrunk from thinking about.

He drew himself to his fullest height, which was a handsome five-foot-eight-and-a-half, and looked down at Myra with a steely glint in his eye, picked up from Clint Eastwood in one of his spaghetti Westerns. "I would kindly request you to refrain from making adverse remarks about my articulation, madame," he said, "when you at your best give the impression of a frog with laryngitis." It was pretty strong stuff for one who had all but plighted his troth, and Myra, a woman of spirit, rose to her feet with blazing eyes.

"If that is your attitude," she said, and there was a Wilkinson sword-edge to her voice, "I would pray trouble you not to pollute this house further with your undesirable presence."

Bobby gave her a strained Calmpose smile. "Very well," he said, "I shall leave now." He was damned if he was going to continue pressing his suit with a woman who was sarcastic, full of insinuations, insulting, and had other preferences anyway. It was with a truly majestic stride, Bobby tells me, that he walked up the stairs to collect his things.

Waiter, another John Collins, if you please.

But after he had hailed the first passing taxi and directed the turbaned charioteer to his Calcutta residence (said Cedric, sipping his fifth) remorse overwhelmed him. He thought of what he had given up because of his foolish pride. So what if a woman was sarcastic, full of insinuations, insulting, and had other preferences anyway, as long as she had what it takes? A minor contender like Rahim Ali could easily have been overcome. Instead he had behaved insufferably—insufferably.

He did not tarry long at his residence. After dumping his bags there Bobby Chatterjee shot like an arrow straight in the direction of the Light Horse Bar, there to drown his sorrows in alcohol. It was sad, very sad—but it was Fate.

While Cedric paused to wipe his eyes at the conclusion of his narrative, I perceived that Bobby had finished his drinking bout and risen to his feet. I thought I might as well toddle along and commiserate. Accordingly, I left the others at the table, and strolled to Bobby.

"I say, Bobby," I said.

"What?" His voice, for one who had been steeped in such sorrow, was surprisingly steady.

"I came to say I heard about Myra, and I want to tell you I'm very sorry. . . ."

"What the devil are you talking about?"

"Myra. . ."

"And who the hell is Myra?"

At first I thought drink had dulled his memory, and then a sneaking suspicion crept into my mind. I turned to look for Cedric: he had just finished his fifth John Collins, at my expense, and was sidling to the door.

"You mean you don't know a girl called Myra?"

"Certainly not."

"Then what was your drinking session in aid of?" Cedric had left the barroom, and the swing door shut soundlessly after him.

"Oh, that . . ." Bobby paused in recollection of his miseries—"I placed a thousand bucks on a hot tip—Happy Boy in the 2:30—and it came seventh. Seventh," he repeated dully. "In a seven-horse race."

He walked unhappily to the door through which Cedric had just passed.

1972

The Village Girl

Sunder had never met a girl like her before. He knew the species existed, of course. At Delhi University the term for its members was *behenjis* (respected sisters), an ironic reference to the fact that no one in his right mind would try to flirt with one. They wore floral-patterned *salwar-kameez* with nylon *dupattas* and scarlet polish was forever flaking off their nails. They also chattered on buses in Hindi or Punjabi and spoke English, if at all, in an accent you could have ground *dal* with. Here in Kerala you had to allow for regional variations of dress and patois, but Sunder could spot a *behenji* at fifty paces, and though the word didn't exist locally in Malayalam, it was clear that a *behenji* was what she was. And, horror of horrors, he was going to be introduced to her.

He stood at the foot of the stairs looking into the long hall that served as salon, dining-room, clothes-drying area, and thoroughfare in the ancestral home, and cursed his lack of alternatives. It was bad enough having nothing to do, which was his usual condition on these annual duty-visits to Kerala. It was decidedly worse having to do something he didn't want to do. His mother had summoned him downstairs to "meet someone your own age."

Knowing his mother, this could easily turn out to be a precocious fourteen-year-old schoolboy who wanted to talk about his stamp collection. Sunder peered around the doorway. The girl sitting with her hands on her lap, next to a white-haired matron of formidable aspect, looked closer to his real age than to his mother's usual estimation of it, but she was certifiably a *behenji*. Making conversation with her was going to be even less stimulating than rereading the dog-eared Conan Doyles he had found in his grandfather's cupboard.

Sunder swore under his breath, but realized there was no escape. He would have to put in an appearance, for politeness' sake. But he would be damned if it was going to be more than a perfunctory one, whatever his mother might say in that reproachful way of hers afterward. "Look, I never wanted to come anyway," he would remonstrate again if she did so. "As far as I'm concerned, this flight to the south every winter is strictly for the birds." She wouldn't get the joke, but there would be no mistaking his message. And they would subside again into the mutually resentful truce that always characterized their relations on these visits.

Every year, without exception, his parents dragged him all the way down to their village homes in Kerala for what they described as a family holiday. This consisted largely of the elders talking interminably to each other about the misfortunes of people Sunder didn't know, or receiving and paying ritual visits to people Sunder didn't want to know. As his adolescence advanced Sunder tried to opt out of the exercise and was firmly told he didn't have an option. "We have to go home," his father explained, "to renew our roots. I may be working in Delhi, but this is where we're from and where we all belong." Sunder bitterly asked once why, if they wanted to renew their roots, *he* had to be uprooted. His father gave him a shocked lecture on the dangers of cultural deracination. "When you're our age," he added, "you'll be grateful we preserved your identity." Sunder's more pertinent arguments—that "home" for him had always been Delhi, where he had grown up, not Kerala, where they had—were overruled without discussion. And so he had to leave his friends and records and motorcycle behind in Delhi to vegetate with his grandparents in Kerala, eat palate-numbing quantities of coconut chutney and attempt to respond in his insufficient Malayalam to predictable gibes about the length of his hair. It was altogether unbearable.

Today Sunder's father was out tramping the countryside in a spotless, cream *mundu*, a pair of thick-soled Bata sandals his only concession to urbanity, catching up on old classmates, while his mother remained "at home" to a miscellaneous collection of distant relatives and nearby acquaintances. Neither activity had appealed to Sunder. He had lain instead on his string-bed, trying with the help of Sherlock Holmes not to think about what he was missing in Delhi. When his mother's summons came, Holmes and he had not been entirely successful.

Curses exhaled, Sunder walked in, making no attempt to conceal his lack of enthusiasm. He felt a stab of perverse satisfaction at his mother's evident disapproval of his sartorial standards. He was defiantly wearing jeans and a fishnet T-shirt, which his father said made him look like the villain's sidekick in a bad Hindi movie. (His father had only ever seen one Hindi movie, but it had been enough to provide him with an endless stock of stereotypes). The girl, however, seemed to regard him with a sort of light in her eyes. Sunder noticed this and exaggerated the indifference with which he dropped into a wooden chair and mumbled his hello.

"Narayani Amma is an old friend of the family, dear," his mother explained, indicating the matron, who favored him with a cursory glance and continued talking in cascading Malayalam at the top of her not inconsiderable voice. Sunder registered that the oration in progress dealt with the marital misfortunes of a number of good-hearted Kerala ladies who all seemed somehow to be related to each other and to the speaker. What a lot of adult delinquents the community had managed to produce, Sunder thought: every one of the ladies mentioned seemed to have married a bounder, a drunkard, a wife-beater, an unemployable idler or a crook unintelligent enough to have been caught with his hand in the till, with the prize unfortunate being the Kollengode woman whose husband had managed to combine in his person every one of these deficiencies.

"Susheela is Narayani Amma's niece," his mother told him by way of introduction to the *behenji* when her visitor paused for breath. "Her mother's sister's son's daughter," she added with the precision she customarily applied to the description of such relationships, as if the extra degree of accuracy would somehow render the encounter more full of meaning for Sunder. He briefly tried to trace the lineage his mother had outlined, gave up, and looked away.

"She has passed her SSLC in the English medium," the formidable aunt announced with pride. "Go on, Susheela, say something in English to Kamala *edathi*." Sunder's mother smiled encouragingly, but Susheela only simpered her embarrassment, twisting her hands in her lap. Sunder rolled his eyes toward the transverse beams on the ceiling. It was going to be even worse than he had feared.

But Narayani Amma was not one to let silences endure. Putting the brief diversion determinedly behind her, she picked up her disquisition where she had left off. Sunder gathered she had now turned the powerful floodlights of her larynx on the dark sins of the younger generation. "You don't know what things are coming to here," she declaimed. "Just as bad as Hollywood, I tell you. Why, in Karanad Chandrika *chechi's* very street in Chittilamchery, well, in the street just behind hers, a Nair girl committed suicide by drinking pesticide. Seems she had been having an affair with, you won't believe this, an Ezhava boy, a common farmhand they wouldn't have allowed into their house. Someone told Chandrika *chechi* the girl found out she was pregnant, but of course she had to be cremated quickly, so no one will ever know. But why talk of

Chittilamchery, things are hardly better in our own backyard. Why, just the other week old Gopan Nair's daughter—you know Gopan Nair, Kallasheri Madhavan Nair's sister's husband, whose brother's son is working for Travancore Chemicals in Madras— well, Gopan Nair's daughter told her parents, after they had arranged her wedding and everything, that she was in love—can you believe it, in *love?*—with a Rauther fellow in her class, a Muslim if you please. Can you imagine? They had to stop sending her to school, of course, and some of the Nair boys got together and gave this Muslim a good beating, and told him it would be worse for him if he ever came near the girl's house again. Apparently he got some sort of labourer's job in the Gulf or somewhere and went away. But poor Gopan Nair, that girl of his is still refusing to marry anyone. . . ."

Sunder stifled a yawn. The world of Narayani Amma's concerns could not have been farther removed from that of his experience. Delhi, at least *his* Delhi, seemed to be on another planet, with its discotheques, its music festivals, its fun-loving chicks who modeled, who acted in plays, whose enameled fingers snaked round his waist to hold him tightly as he raced his motorcycle down Ring Road. . . . He broke into what was becoming a self-indulgent reverie and looked at Susheela. She quickly averted her own gaze. *Behenji* she clearly was, in her adolescent *pavada* and *davani*, the long skirt ensemble with a half-sari-look worn by teenage Malayali damsels. Her nails were clipped and unpolished, her face devoid of makeup except for the film of talcum powder patted on by every rural Keralite, her feet bare (Sunder had no doubt he would find a pair of blue rubber thongs deferentially slipped off outside the front door). Otherwise, Sunder had to grant she was pretty in a typically Malayali way, all kohl-rimmed eyes and dimples and long black tresses that wore the sheen of years of diligent oiling. He wrinkled his nose at the thought of all that oil. In Delhi he wouldn't have given her a second look. He'd be damned if he would in Kerala either.

Narayani Amma was holding forth now on the moral standards, or lack of them, of a particularly winsome Vallenghy schoolgirl whom she swore she had personally, with her own eyes, seen in a movie theater with a boy who was not her brother. "It's all this education these girls are getting these days. All they know about right and wrong is what they need to pass their exams. Nothing else. I tell you, Kamala, it is all the fault of this Communist government. The moment they insisted on free and compulsory education, I could see it coming. . . ."

This is where I quit, Sunder decided. Not that they'll miss me. He rose abruptly from his seat with a muttered "excuse me" designed not to interrupt the visitor's conversational flow. Feeling in his hip pocket for his crushed pack of concealed Panama cigarettes, he strode towards the veranda that skirted the house. "Sunder," his mother's voice called out, "if you're going for a walk, why don't you take Susheela with you and show her the garden?"

He stopped short as if he had been lassoed and turned in irritation towards his mother. She had always had an uncanny instinct for the inconvenient. "For Christ's sake" were the words springing to his lips when he caught sight of Susheela's face. There was something in her expression—part awe, part delight, part anticipation, part nervousness—that changed his mind. "Oh, all right, come along then," he said, and without waiting for her he crossed the threshold.

After a few paces, Sunder stood on a corner of the veranda and looked out onto the paddies stretching into the distance. Dusk was descending with the rapidity of the latitude, the sunlight curling off the edges of the sky. The palm trees bordering the far end of the rice fields were beginning to darken in the shadowy embrace of the approaching twilight. It was still, the quiet broken only by the screech of unidentifiable insects. He sensed rather than saw the girl's silent approach and looked down to acknowledge her presence beside him. She was standing, her mouth partly open in nervous excitement, and Sunder found his perception of the girl widening to take in two more details. First, she was even shorter than he had guessed: she came barely up to his shoulders. Second, her figure, concealed by the *davani* but no longer distorted by her sitting posture, was as close to female perfection as he had ever seen.

"Come on," he said in some confusion, "I'll show you the garden." Without waiting for a response he walked down the steps that led from the veranda to the dusty yard surrounding the house. The traditional fruit trees stood around the yard—mango, jackfruit, banana, all serving a functional rather than aesthetic purpose—but that was quite typical, and not what his mother had meant him to display. What was special in this house was that one corner of the yard had been miraculously brought to life and, unusually for these parts, sustained grass and blooming flowerbeds. The family was inordinately proud of this triumph over both nature and custom.

"That's it," he announced redundantly with a general wave of the hand, not quite knowing how to go about showing a girl a garden.

"It is beautiful," she said simply, and Sunder realized in surprise that these were the first words he had heard her speak. He could almost imagine her reciting the "Yinglish" sounds from a list of phonemes in Malayalam script. "What those flowers are called?"

She was pointing to a cluster of bright yellow blossoms. "I haven't a clue," he admitted. "And I couldn't name anything else in the garden either," he added hastily. She laughed, a musical tinkle, and Sunder felt disarmed rather than offended. "Then there is not much point in showing the garden, isn't it?" she asked softly. "Would it not be better to simply sit and talk, Sunder *etta*?"

Sunder *etta*! Ironic transference: the *behenji* had gone and made an elder brother out of him! That was, of course, the Kerala custom: it would be disrespectful of her to call him by his name. "Sure, if you like," he found himself saying. "But forget about this *etta* business, Susheela. I'm only nineteen, for Christ's sake."

"And I am only seventeen," she replied shyly. "But I am becoming eighteen next month. That is my star birthday, you know, according to our Malayalam calendar, not my date birthday." She was flushing, as if she had said too much. "Sunder *etta*, may I ask you something?"

"Sure," he replied uneasily. This was going to be like no conversation he had ever had. Conversing as an *etta* to a village *behenji* in primary school English was going to be, he reflected, a whole new scene.

"Sunder *etta*, what is the meaning of this expression you are using: for Christ's sake?"

Sunder laughed. "Meaning? It doesn't really *mean* anything, for Christ's sake, it's just an expression . . ."

"And you are just using it again," Susheela giggled.

"Look, it's just a way of saying, you know, emphasizing something. Haven't you heard of the expression "for God's sake?" It's the same thing—God, Christ, what's the difference?"

"But you are not Christian," she objected simply. "Are you, Sunder *etta*?"

"No, I'm not," he replied, looking at her in some exasperation. They had reached the spot he had intended to escape to when he rose from his chair, a sheltered part of the veranda of the storehouse, out of sight of the main house itself, where he safely smoked the surreptitious cigarettes he still could not light in front of his family. "But that's not really relevant, see? You don't have to be Christian. It's just an English expression. You don't have to be English to talk English, right?"

"Yes, I see," she nodded, as they settled on the smooth, stone floor. "But it is all very strange to me. Like you're always saying 'sorry' and 'thank you' in English."

"What's wrong with saying sorry and thank you?" he asked, fishing for his cigarettes.

"Nothing, of course, but it is not Indian," she said. "We are not having any word for 'sorry' and 'thank you' in Malayalam language. In our culture you are supposed to show your—sorrow, or your gratefulness—gratitude, by your normal actions and expressions. This English way, it is as if one or two words are enough to pay your debt. Isn't it?"

Sunder had found his pack. "I guess I haven't thought about it that way," he admitted, taking out a cigarette.

"You see, you are not really Malayali anymore." She drew in her own breath at her boldness and asked anxiously, "I hope I am not, how do you say, offending you, Sunder *etta*?" He shook his head, smiling. "But really, it is very English there, in the city, isn't it? I mean Western. Modern. Like England and America."

"Hardly," Sunder began, then wondered. "Well, perhaps, in a certain way. Hey, do you mind if I smoke?"

"No, of course not, Sunder *etta*," the girl said. Sunder leaned against the wall, lighting a cigarette in his cupped hands. He shook the match out, and the gesture sent scudding shadows across the girl's attentive face. It did not occur to him to offer her one: it was inconceivable that she would smoke. "In what way, Sunder *etta*?"

"In what way?" Sunder looked at her and saw a beautiful girl, no longer nervous, at his feet. Her expression, laden with curiosity and interest, drove any coherent answer out of his mind. "What do you mean, in what way?"

"I mean, in what way is your life in the city like the foreign countries?" For once her words were halting. "I can see you are so modern, Sunder *etta*. Here in the village I am knowing nothing of the kind of life you are leading in the big city. It must be so different. Please describe it to me, Sunder *etta*. I am really wanting to know."

"Aw, it isn't all that dramatic, Susheela," Sunder replied. "But haven't you been to a city? Not Delhi, perhaps, but Bombay? Madras?" She shook her head. "Not even Cochin?"

"I have never left the district, Sunder *etta*. The farthest I have ever gone anywhere was to the Guruvayoor temple, with my Amma." That, Sunder knew, was about two hours from the village by bus: he had had to make the same trip a few times. "Why would I be going to a city? My father is a *marsh* in the village, a schoolteacher."

"But don't you have any relatives in Bombay or Madras? Or someone to visit on a holiday?"

She shook her head silently, and Sunder knew that holidays meant even less to her than this one did to him; in fact they meant nothing at all. You could not travel very far on a village schoolteacher's pay. "Heck, I'd better tell you then, huh?" he suggested lightly. "Big buildings—lots of cars, crowds, concrete. No rice fields! Water out of taps and not out of a well. Telephones . . ." The nearest telephone connection was in a town eighteen miles away. Sunder went on, describing stereo systems, air-conditioning, chewing gum, television (Delhi was the only Indian city with TV, so though no one in his right mind watched the boring black-and-white documentaries it offered, it was worth boasting about). As the girl soaked it all in in wide-eyed appreciation, he became more expansive, taking in the University Coffee House and the Houses of Parliament, the sound system at the Cellar, the foreign dignitaries visiting Rashtrapati Bhavan. Her wonder about the city then focused on him as its principal inhabitant. The questions became more personal: what did he eat for breakfast? Did he know how to drive? What did he smoke? Did he have girlfriends? What were his plans after college? He spoke airily of not being able to decide between management studies and taking the Foreign Service exams, and spoke with intellectual disdain of the cocktail circuit that both would condemn him to. Had he stepped out of a spaceship on Mars he could not have been greeted with more avid, and admiring, curiosity. Each answer, each trivial detail, seemed to elevate him in her esteem; he was unique, her sole means of intimate access to a world she knew existed but with which she had no contact. And yet, Sunder realized even as he spoke, the access he offered was entirely illusory: she lacked the framework, the knowledge, the vocabulary to translate what he was saying into terms she could relate to and evaluate. She had heard, but she had not really understood.

"What do *you* do?" he found himself asking. "I mean, you've finished school, right? Are you going to college now?"

"I—no, I am not going to college," she replied in a low voice, looking down at the floor as if ashamed of her answer. "I did well in my SSLC, but my father—my father, he does not believe in college education for me." She shook her head violently. "It is not his fault, he can only afford the fees for one child and my brother is more important, he is doing B.S. in agriculture. Everyone says the future is in that. It is costing a lot, my brother has failed twice already, and there are the hostel fees and all. What is a girl going to do with a college degree anyway, my Amma says, will it help me make better *idlis* for my husband?"

"But your father's a schoolteacher!" Sunder protested. "Surely he doesn't go along with that?"

The girl said nothing. Then, for the first time since he had asked the question, she looked directly at him. "He says a girl has to graduate from homework to housework," she said quietly. "I am getting married next month. The week after my star birthday."

Sunder did not know how to react. Married! She was seventeen, barely out of petticoats. His instincts told him to show how appalled he was; his conditioning impelled him in the opposite direction. "Congratulations," he said formally, wondering if that was another word for which there existed no Malayalam equivalent.

"They arranged everything," she went on in an emotionless

tone of voice. "He came with his family to inspect—to see me, last month. I wore a sari for the first time and served them *dosas* I had made with my own hands. They said yes."

"And you? Did you like him?"

"He is thin and dark, with pencil-line moustache. His two front teeth stick out a bit. It was 4:30 in the afternoon, but I could smell arrack on his breath. He was married before, his last wife died, no one is knowing how exactly. He has small child from her, a two-year-old girl."

"But why do your parents want you to marry someone like that?"

"Because of all this—these—circumstances, his family is not asking for any dowry. They are only wanting a good, homely bride who can cook and look after the house and the little girl. It is a good family, known to my maternal uncle. And he is holding government job, clerk in the Collector's office. Everyone is saying we are very lucky."

"And what do you feel about all this?" Sunder felt deracinated urban outrage welling up in him as he stubbed out the half-smoked cigarette. "Eh?" She would not answer. Avoiding his accusatory eyes, she looked down at the floor. Unthinkingly, he put a hand under her chin and lifted her face to meet his gaze. "Are *you* happy about this?" he asked.

Her eyes glistened. "With my SSLC marks I was elgib— eligible for University scholarship," she said tonelessly. "I only had to submit application. I filled it in, got all certificates from school. Only thing I needed was my father's signature. I took the papers to him, I said look *Achan*, look what your daughter can do, it will not even be costing anything. He took the forms from me and said, very sadly, so Susheela, you want to go study for four years. Then tell me, who will be marrying you four years from now? Will we again find someone from good family, with secure job, and without dowry? These are dreams, child, it is time to wake up. And he tore up the forms."

Sunder struggled with anger and impotence, and anger about his impotence. "They can't do this!" he burst out, knowing even as he spoke the words that they were absurd. Of course they could do this: it was what millions of Indian families did.

He saw the tears slowly overflow her eyes and begin to trickle down her cheeks. Helplessly, one hand still holding up her chin, he raised the other to her face to wipe away the tears. With a sudden movement she caught it and kissed his palm. Soft lips pressed against the hot wetness of her own tears, and Sunder's free hand fell startled from her chin. It was not a conscious motion, and it should have simply fallen to his side, but it did not. It fell upon her breast, and after that there was nothing anymore he could do to prevent what happened.

Neither of them spoke a word. When they had rearranged their clothes and begun to walk back to the house in silence, it was dark. There were a hundred things Sunder wanted to say, but he was too suffused with guilt and shame to find the words. It was, of course, all his fault. He, the experienced city slicker, he with the smooth talk and the plastic fantasies and the fishnet T-shirt, had cynically taken advantage of an innocent village girl. She had sought admission to his world, and he had taken her body. True, he could recall no resistance to his caresses, but the girl was probably too surprised to resist and too ingenuous to know how to. In the dark he had not really been able to see her face, but her silence was plain enough. He had ruined her. He had destroyed the illusions of a simple village girl, a nervous, trusting young thing who called him Sunder *etta*.

They reached the veranda of the main house. In a few steps they would be at the doorway of the living room, and it would be too late to say anything. He could not leave everything unsaid, even if expiation was impossible. He caught her by the arm and, in a strangulated voice, spoke the only words that occurred to him.

"I'm sorry," he said.

She had taken the first step from the yard to the porch and the moonlight suddenly bathed her face. It was lit up in the radiance of dreams fulfilled, and her smile was no longer that of a nervous girl, but of a woman who had touched a happiness she had not expected to be hers.

A cloud passed, but Sunder found himself grateful for the darkness.

"Thank you," she said. "Thank you—Sunder."

1972

City Girl

Sundari, known to her friends and intimates at Delhi University as Sandy, hated being in her grandfather's house in Kerala. She hated even more having to pretend she didn't hate it. And since she had been summoned downstairs by her mother for a bout of obligatory socializing with the rural masses, that was just what she would have to do.

Sandy stood at the foot of the stairs looking into the long hall, which served as salon, dining room, clothes-drying area, and thoroughfare in the ancestral home, and cursed her lack of alternatives. It was bad enough having nothing to do, which was her usual condition on these annual duty-visits to Kerala. It was decidedly worse having to do something she didn't want to do. In calling out to her, her mother had said she would "meet someone your own age." Knowing Mummy, this could easily turn out to be a precocious fourteen-year-old schoolboy who wanted to talk about his stamp collection. Sandy peered around the doorway. The youth sitting on the bench against the wall, next to a white-haired matron of formidable aspect, looked closer to her real age than to her mother's usual estimation of it, but he was certifiably a *dehati*, a village type. Making conversation with him, assuming they had ten words in common, was going to be even less stimulating than rereading the dog-eared Agatha Christies she had found in her grandfather's cupboard.

Sandy swore in a most unladylike way under her breath, but realized there was no escape. She would have to put in an appearance, for politeness' sake. But she would be damned if it was going to be more than a perfunctory one, whatever her mother might say in that reproachful way of hers afterward. What did Mummy think she could possibly have to say to this son of the soil? And if her parents thought Sandy rude she'd remind them she had never wanted to come anyway. "As far as I'm concerned," she would say acidly, "this flight to the south every winter is strictly for the birds." Mummy wouldn't get the joke, but there would be no mistaking its message. And they would subside again into the mutually resentful truce that always characterized their relations on these visits.

Every year, without exception, her parents dragged her all the way down to their village homes in Kerala for what they described as a family holiday. This consisted largely of the elders talking interminably to each other about the misfortunes of people Sandy didn't know, or receiving and paying ritual visits to people Sandy didn't want to know. As her adolescence advanced Sandy tried to opt out of the exercise and was firmly told she didn't have the option. "We have to go home," her father explained, "to renew our roots. I may be working in Delhi, but this is where we're from and where we all belong." Once Sandy bitterly asked why, if they wanted to renew their roots, *she* had to be uprooted. Her father gave her a shocked lecture on the dangers of cultural deracination. "When you're our age," he added, "you'll be grateful we preserved your identity." Sandy's more pertinent arguments — that "home" for her had always been Delhi, where she had grown up, not Kerala, where they had — were overruled without discussion. And so she had to leave her friends and records and favorite haunts behind in Delhi to vegetate with her grandparents in Kerala, eat palate-numbing quantities of coconut chutney, and attempt to respond in her insufficient Malayalam to predictable gibes about the "boyish" cut of her hair. It was altogether unbearable.

Today Sandy's father was out tramping the countryside in a spotless cream *mundu*, a pair of thick-soled Bata sandals his only concession to urbanity, catching up on old classmates, while her mother remained "at home" to a miscellaneous collection of distant relatives and nearby acquaintances. The first activity had vaguely appealed to Sandy, but her father had made it clear that her presence would make him most uncomfortable. So she had stayed at home, not holding court by her mother's side but lying instead on her string-bed, trying with the help of Hercule Poirot not to think about what she was missing in Delhi. When her mother's summons came, Poirot and she had not been entirely successful.

Curses exhaled, Sandy walked in, making no attempt to conceal her lack of enthusiasm. She felt a stab of perverse satisfaction at her mother's evident disapproval of her sartorial standards. She was defiantly wearing jeans and a tee-shirt, both of which clung to her body in a way that made her look, or so her father had disgustedly claimed, like the subsidiary vamp in a bad Hindi movie. (Her father had seen only one Hindi movie, but it had been enough to provide him with an endless stock of stereotypes.) The youth, however, seemed to regard her with a sort of light in his eyes. Sandy noticed this and exaggerated the indifference with which she dropped into a wooden chair and mumbled her hello.

"Narayani Amma is an old friend of the family, dear," her mother explained, indicating the matron, who favored her with a cursory glance and continued talking in cascading Malayalam at the top of her not inconsiderable voice. Sandy registered that the oration in progress dealt with the marital misfortunes of a number of good-hearted Kerala ladies who all seemed somehow to be related to each other and to the speaker. What a lot of adult delinquents the community had managed to produce, Sandy thought: every one of the ladies mentioned seemed to have married a bounder, a drunkard, a wife-beater, an unemployable idler, or a crook unintelligent enough to have been caught with his hand in the till, with the prize unfortunate being the Kollengode woman whose husband had managed to combine in his person every one of these deficiencies.

"Shantakumar is Narayani-Amma's nephew," her mother told her by way of introduction to the *dehati* when her visitor paused for breath. "Her mother's sister's daughter's son," she added with the precision she customarily applied to the description of such relationships, as if the extra degree of accuracy would somehow render the encounter more full of meaning for Sandy. She briefly tried to trace the lineage her mother had outlined, gave up, and looked away.

"Shantan has passed his SSLC in the English medium," the formidable aunt announced with pride. "Go on, boy, say something in English to Kamala *edathi*." Sandy's mother smiled encouragingly, but Shantakumar just cleared his throat in embarrassment, his hands holding the edge of the bench so tightly the veins stood up on them. Sandy rolled her eyes toward the transverse beams on the ceiling. It was going to be even worse than she had feared.

But Narayani Amma was not one to let silences endure. Putting the brief diversion determinedly behind her, she picked up her disquisition where she had left off. Sandy gathered she had now turned the powerful floodlights of her larynx on the dark sins of the younger generation. "You don't know what things are coming to here," she declaimed. "Just as bad as Hollywood, I tell you. Why, in Karanad Chandrika *chechi*'s very street in Chittilamchery, well in the street just behind hers, a Nair girl committed suicide by drinking pesticide. Seems she had been having an affair with, you won't believe this, an Ezhava boy, a common farmhand they wouldn't have allowed into their house. Someone told Chandrika-chechi the girl found out she was pregnant, but of course she had to be cremated quickly, so no one will ever know. But why talk of Chittilamchery, things are hardly better in our own backyard. Why, just the other week old Gopan Nair's daughter — you know Gopan Nair, Kallasheri Madhavan Nair's sister's husband, whose brother's son is working for Travancore Chemicals in Madras — well, Gopan Nair's daughter told her parents, after they had arranged her wedding and everything, that she was in love — can you believe it, in *love*? — with a Rauther fellow in her class, a Muslim if you please. Can you imagine? They had to stop sending her to school, of course, and some of the Nair boys got together and gave this Muslim a good beating, and told him it would be worse for him if he ever came near the girl's house again. Apparently he got some sort of laborer's job in the Gulf or somewhere and went away. But poor Gopan Nair, that girl of his is still refusing to marry anyone. . . ."

Sandy stifled a yawn. The world of Narayani-Amma's concerns could not have been farther removed from that of her experience. Delhi, at least *her* Delhi, seemed to be on another planet, with its discotheques, its music festivals, its fun opportunities to model, to act in plays, to race down Ring Road on the back of Chippie's motorcycle with her arms around his waist. . . . She broke into what was becoming a self-indulgent reverie and looked at Shan-takumar, who quickly averted his own gaze. *Dehati* he clearly was, a short strong dark figure of a youth clad in a whitish *mundu*, the long untailored waistcloth that served as all-purpose attire for Malayali males. His simple cotton shirt was a size too small, the collar noticeably frayed from too many washes. His feet were bare and the rough, stubby toes had clearly known many a trudge through the rice paddies. Sandy had no doubt she would find a pair of blue rubber thongs deferentially slipped off outside the front door. The boy's short, diligently oiled hair was combed backward. Sandy wrinkled her nose at the thought of all that oil. She thought of Chippie, elegant Chippie with his V-shaped denim jackets and the Gucci boots his mother had brought him from Italy. This Shantan (what kind of name was that anyway for a guy?) couldn't even be thought of in the same breath.

Narayani Amma was holding forth now on the amorality of a particularly winsome Vallenghy schoolgirl whom she swore she had personally, with her own eyes, seen in a movie theater with a boy who was not her brother. "It's all this education these girls are getting these days. All they know about right and wrong is what they need to pass their exams. Nothing else. I tell you, Kamala, it is all the fault of this Communist government. The moment they insisted on free and compulsory education, I could see it coming. . . ."

This is where I quit, Sandy decided. Not that they'll miss me. She rose abruptly from her seat with a muttered "excuse me" designed not to interrupt the visitor's conversational flow. Feeling in her hip pocket for her crushed pack of concealed Charms cigarettes, she strode toward the verandah that skirted the house. "Sundari," her mother's voice called out, "where are you going?"

She stopped short as if she had been lassoed and turned in irritation toward her mother. Mummy always had an uncanny instinct for the inconvenient. "Just for a walk, Mummy," she said. "I thought I might go up to the temple and perhaps do the twilight *arati*," she added maliciously. Her mother knew what she really thought of religion.

"It's not safe walking around like that, Sundari dear, especially since it's getting dark," her mother responded with, Sandy thought, equal malice. "Why don't you take young Shantan with you for company?"

Sandy bit her lip. "In that case," she was about to say, "I'd rather not go at all," but she caught sight of Shantan's face and the words dried on her tongue. There was something in his expression — part delight, part anticipation, part nervousness — that changed her mind. "Oh, all right, come along then," she said, and without waiting for him she crossed the threshold.

After a few paces, Sandy stood on a corner of the verandah and looked out on the paddies stretching into the distance. Dusk was descending with the rapidity of the latitude, the sunlight curling off the edges of the sky. The palm trees bordering the far end of the rice fields were beginning to darken in the shadowy embrace of the approaching twilight. It was still, the quiet broken only by the screak of unidentifiable insects. She sensed rather than saw the youth's silent approach, padding across the verandah on his bare feet. Sandy turned to acknowledge Shantan's presence beside her. Standing, the boy was almost a head shorter than she, and Sandy found herself looking down on him in more ways than one. But there was no doubting the physical strength packed into the youth's stocky frame; pectoral muscles bulged under the too-tight shirt, and as he lifted his mundu to his knees in a *pimbadi* to free his legs for the walk, Shantan bared dark calves more muscular than Sandy had ever seen.

"Come on," she said in some confusion, "let's go." Without waiting for a response, she walked down the steps that led from the verandah to the dusty yard surrounding the house. The boy silently followed. Halfway across the yard Sandy's steps faltered. She hesitated, unable to decide between the back gate that led toward the village and the side gate that opened onto the rice fields and would eventually take her to the main road. After a brief pause she turned, and the youth said in calm but heavily accented English, "That is not way to temple."

Sandy realized in surprise that these were the first words she had heard him speak. "Yes, I know," she said, feeling the initiative slip away from her.

"Then why you are walking that way?" Shantan asked simply.

"I haven't a clue," she admitted. "I guess I don't really want to go to the temple." The boy's brow wrinkled in puzzlement, and

Sandy felt ashamed of her deception. "I'm sorry," she added. "Thank you for coming along anyway."

"No mention, Sundari *chechi*," the boy replied, gutturally gracious.

Chechi! Shantan was calling her "elder sister." That was, of course, the Kerala custom: it would be disrespectful of him to address her by her name. "You mean 'don't mention it,' " she corrected him with the weight of age and education on her side. "And while you're about it, don't mention this *chechi* business either, for Christ's sake. We're practically the same age, aren't we?"

The boy digested this suggestion, his small eyes with their dark black pupils still. "How old are you, Sundari *chechi*?" he asked matter-of-factly.

"Nineteen," she replied, disarmed by his directness. "And you?"

"I will be eighteen next month," he answered. "But according to my school certificate, I am same age as you. My father changed my date of birth to get me admission sooner. They were having too many children in the house, and I am always getting in the way."

She laughed, not so much at what he had said but at the gravity with which he said it. "Then you really must drop the *chechi*."

"As you wish, Sundari *chechi*," he said, tilting his head sideways and down in that confusing Keralite nod that always left Northerners uncertain as to whether acquiescence or disagreement was intended.

"No *chechi*, for Christ's sake," she insisted firmly, still laughing. "And my friends all call me Sandy."

His somber eyes took that in with a flicker, as if uncertain what to do with the information. They were standing in the middle of the yard, the setting sun in her eyes. "Shall we go and sit down somewhere?" she asked, to her own surprise.

"Of course, if you like," she heard him saying, and wondered how on earth she had got herself into a position where the very last thing she would have wanted to do — sit and talk to a bloody *dehati*, for Christ's sake — was "what *she* liked"! At least his English was better than she had expected. "Sundari *chechi*, I mean Sandy, may I ask you something?"

"Sure," she replied uneasily. This was going to be like no conversation she had ever had. Guys like Shantan were completely peripheral to her consciousness: one knew they existed but one never actually met them, let alone talked to them. And now here she was, asking him to sit down with her. Boy, did she need a cigarette. She walked on, the youth, still barefoot, close behind.

"Sandy" — he said it slowly, as if tasting the unfamiliar sound to test it — "what is the meaning of this expression you are using: for Christ's sake?"

Sandy laughed. "Meaning? It doesn't really *mean* anything, for Christ's sake, it's just an expression . . ."

"And you are just using it again," Shantan pointed out.

"Look, it's just a way of saying, you know, emphasizing something. Haven't you heard of the expression 'for God's sake'? It's the same thing — God, Christ, what's the difference?"

"But you are not Christian," he objected simply. "Are you, Sunda — Sandy?"

"No, I'm not," she replied, looking at him in some exasperation. They had reached the spot she had intended to escape to when she rose from the chair, a sheltered part of the verandah of the storehouse, out of sight of the main house itself, where she safely smoked the surreptitious cigarettes she still could not light in front of her family. "But that's not really relevant, see? You don't have to be Christian. It's just an English expression. You don't have to be English to talk English, right? I mean, look at you."

"Yes, I see," Shantan said, as they settled on the smooth stone floor. "But it is all very strange to me. Like you are always saying 'sorry' and 'thank you' in English."

"What's wrong with saying sorry and thank you?" she asked, fishing for her cigarettes.

"Nothing, I suppose, but it is not Indian," he said. "We are not having any word for 'sorry' and 'thank you' in Malayalam language. In our culture you are supposed to show you are sorry, or thankful, by your normal actions and expressions. This English way, it is as if one-two words are enough to pay your debt. No?"

"Yes, I suppose so," Sandy said, taking out a cigarette. "I guess I haven't thought about it that way."

"You see, you are not really Malayali anymore, Sandy." This time the name was used much more deliberately, as if Shantan had considered the label and determined it fitted. Was it her imagination, or was he eyeing her cigarette with hostility? "You are all very English there, in the city, isn't it? I mean Westernish. Modern. Like the English and Americans."

"Hardly," Sandy began, then wondered. "Well, perhaps, in a certain way. Hey, do you mind if I smoke?"

"You should not smoke," the youth said gravely.

Sandy leaned against the wall, dismayed. "I know, I know, all this stuff about cancer, right?" she said. "But I just smoke two or three a day, you know, it's not going to kill me." She began lighting the cigarette in her cupped hands.

"It is not that," Shantan replied, as she shook the match out, sending scudding shadows across his expressionless face. "It is wrong for lady to smoke. In Indian culture, you would be being considered bad woman."

Sandy's eyes widened in astonishment, an astonishment deepened by shock and embarrassment as the boy casually plucked the cigarette from her fingers and stubbed it out on the floor. "Better this way," he said quietly.

Her mouth had literally dropped open. A thousand exclamations jostled for voice in her throat. What the hell did this guy think he was doing? Who in blazes did he think he was? What the ef gave him the right? Not one of her peers in Delhi, of either gender, could have dared presume to do such a thing. And this bloody stunted *dehati*— But she was too angry to articulate any of this, and rage as well as a half-inhaled first puff started her coughing. Even as she spluttered for air her head cleared. He would not understand, and if she made a scene it would all just get back to her parents. After all, if she had the sense not to smoke in front of her elders, she had to have the sense not to do it in front of others with the same attitude. She wasn't any the less furious, but she had to behave her age.

She stopped coughing, and looked at him through watery eyes. He was studying her intently, his normally impassive face wearing an expression of sympathy and curiosity. But the expected words of solicitude did not emerge: he just sat there, head cocked to one side, looking at her. "I'm all right, thanks for asking," she said at last, her voice heavy with irony and suppressed anger.

He was oblivious to the undertones. "You will feel better soon," he said quietly. "You see, these things are not meant for us."

She felt the rage welling up within her again. "What do you know about it?" she asked. "Living here in the village, do you have a clue about life in the great big world outside? I mean, where do you get all your smug certainties from, for Christ's sake?"

His eyes became troubled, and she felt instantly ashamed of her outburst. "I am knowing nothing much about your modern city life," he admitted softly. "But I am knowing about real India, Indian society and culture. I am knowing who I am, Sandy. Are you knowing who you are?"

"Sure I know who I am," she replied in some heat. "What makes you so cocksure, for Christ's sake? What do you know about me? What makes you think I don't know who I am?"

His gaze never shifted. "You are a girl," he said levelly, "but you are dressing like a boy. You are old enough for being married, but your clothes are not . . . modest." He uttered the last word with great care, and Sandy felt the color mount to her cheeks. "You are smoking without your parents knowing about it. And you are having boyfriends, isn't it?"

Sandy found outrage battling embarrassment in her mind. Outrage won. The little semiliterate twerp, how dare he stand in judgment on her like that? "What the hell business is it of yours, anyway?" she blazed back.

He refused to be intimidated. "I am only answering your own question," he said calmly. "You asked me what I am knowing about you. In the village I am knowing nothing of the kind of life you are leading in the big city. But I am hearing a lot, from friends who have visited such places as Bombay and Madras. And I am reading also. Isn't it like this, Sandy? Cigarettes and dancing and boyfriends? And drugs, no?"

"I don't take drugs," Sandy replied hotly, and realized the debate had shifted to his ground. "Well, nothing more than a joint or two, anyway. Look, so what if I smoke and have a boyfriend? Life is different in the city. You don't realize that India isn't just the narrow little confines of your precious village. India is also a city like New Delhi. Big buildings, Shantan, not little huts where everyone knows everyone else. Millions of people, of all kinds. Lots of cars, crowds, concrete. Water out of taps and not out of a well. Telephones . . ." The nearest telephone connection here was in a town eighteen miles away. "I mean, man, it's a different *world* out there. For you it's a big thing to go to Palghat to see a two-year-old movie. In Delhi we have TV — television, that brings pictures from around the world right into our living rooms." (Sandy never watched the boring black-and-white documentaries that constituted Delhi's staple television fare, but that was another matter.) "I'm breathing a completely different air, don't you see? So what if I have boyfriends — I'm not going to come back to the village for a piddly old arranged marriage, understand? Your values, your village society"—she mimicked his accent for those two words— "are fine for you, if you like them, but they don't matter a damn as far as I'm concerned. In the city I'm free, see? So I don't give a shit for your judgments. I don't care what you think, Shantan. Why don't you put *that* in your pipe and smoke it?" Somewhat surprised by her own anger, she pulled out the pack of cigarettes again, and found her hand was trembling.

Calm down, Sandy, she told herself. He means no harm. He just hasn't met anyone like me, that's all. I'm unique, his sole means of intimate access to a world he knows exists but can never hope to have real contact with. You can't blame the guy, she thought, for his attitude: he's only attempting to translate this contact into terms he can relate to and evaluate. He was just trying to understand her, and she should help him, not blow her top.

This time he didn't try to stop her smoking. Her eyes were still on the cigarette she was lighting when she heard him ask, "Are you virgin?"

For a moment she thought she couldn't have heard right, then she realized that of course she had. She fought to control herself: it would do no good to get angry, his skin was thicker than the soles of her Kohlapuri chappals. It was time to stand up for herself, to defend her sense of what she was without shame or submission. Sandy looked directly at her questioner. She did not know what exactly she expected to see in his expression: condemnation perhaps, hostility, or mere prurient curiosity. Instead she found something for which she was completely unprepared.

"No," she found herself admitting in some confusion. Pulling herself together, she added firmly: "Of course not. I'm nineteen, for Christ's sake."

He flinched visibly. Sandy perversely felt it was time to turn the tables on him. "Are you?" she asked, taking a deep puff.

He did not answer. "This man," he asked in a voice devoid of emotion, "is he going to marry you, Sandy?"

"Which man?" Sandy asked, exhaling the smoke and feeling it relax her. She was beginning to enjoy this: she was in control at last.

"You are knowing what I mean. This man who — who made you not a virgin."

"Oh, *him?*" she laughed carelessly. "I stopped seeing him a year ago. I certainly wouldn't marry him, not that he'd ask me."

"Then why . . . why . . ." Shantan's voice trailed off: he was really uncomfortable, the little bugger.

"Why did I sleep with him, you mean?" She asked with deliberate casualness, enjoying watching him squirm. "Oh, I don't know. I guess to find out what it was like."

He said nothing, but she could see the shadow that had fallen across his face.

"Shocked you, have I? Poor Shantan." She took his hand in hers, very much the experienced elder sister. "Look, your reactions are all wrong. You're part of *my* generation, for Christ's sake. You shouldn't be thinking, and sounding, like somebody's parent."

He did not react, and looked down at his hand in hers. "And what it was like?" he asked. "You . . . liked it?"

Sandy began to feel uncomfortable again. "Oh, sure," she tossed the words aside with a shake of her head. "Doesn't everybody?"

"And your boyfriend, the one you are having now," Shantan asked earnestly, "is he not minding?"

"Chippie?" Sandy laughed. "Of course he doesn't mind. He thinks a girl should be experienced. More experienced than I was, in fact." She looked Shantan in the eyes, willing him to understand that there were other ways of thinking about these things than his. "Men do, you know. Come on, Shantan, stop looking as if I've just come from Sodom or something. Grow up."

"And this . . . Chippie," Shantan persisted. "Is he going to marry you?"

"Oh, I don't know," Sandy said. "We haven't talked about it. I guess there'd be problems: he's Muslim, actually, and his parents would probably have a fit. But who the hell thinks about marriage, at our age? Chippie's not even through with college yet."

"At your age," Shantan said, "my sister was already having two children."

Sandy looked at him, at his accusatory eyes, and suddenly felt her holding his hand had changed from the elder-sisterly gesture she had meant it to be. She dropped his hand, and his gaze fell; he looked down at the floor as if unable to meet her eyes. Unthinkingly, she put her fingers under his chin and lifted his face to meet her gaze. "Don't you see," she asked, her eyes dripping patient wisdom, "how different it all is?"

With a sudden movement he caught the raised hand and kissed her palm. Taken completely aback, Sandy stared at him in immobile astonishment. And then his mouth was upon hers.

He had no idea what he was doing: the kiss was hungry but inexpert. For a second Sandy felt the sweetness of his breath and allowed herself to register the unaccustomed flavor of being kissed by a nonsmoker. Then she twisted her mouth away from his and tried to pull herself away from him. He would not let her go, holding her upper arms in an immensely powerful grip that tightened as she struggled to free herself. "Stop it!" she breathed. "What do you think you're—" And then his insistent mouth found her lips again, and she could not speak. She tried to push him away, but he was too strong. She kicked him, but with the force of his body he simply pressed her legs more tightly against the wall. At last it occurred to her. The lit cigarette was still in her left hand. She jabbed upward and outward with it. He jerked back with a stifled sound; his grip slackened and she flung herself away from him.

"Have you gone mad?" she asked, panting.

He looked from her to the small round hole where her cigarette had burned its way through his shirt to singe his midriff. "Why did you do that?" he asked.

"Why—why did I—?" Sandy shook her head in wonder. "Boy, you're really something, aren't you, Shantan? You throw yourself on me, practically trying to rape me, and you ask me why I tried to stop you?"

"You did not want me to kiss you." It was a statement, not a question.

Sandy looked at him. She saw the taut, well-muscled body, heard the resentment in the quiet voice, and imagined the unspoken charge: "So I'm not good enough for you?" Of course he wasn't, but how could one tell him that? She could imagine him thinking, she's not even a virgin, why does she push me away? Oh, Shantan, just because I'm not married and I sleep with someone, it doesn't mean I'm willing to sleep with anyone: how could she tell him that? How could she tell him *any*thing? She should never have placed herself in this impossible position.

He took a step toward her. "This Muslim Chippie," he said. "I suppose he is more handsome than me. He is making love to you in better English. Whereas I am only ignorant village boy. So what if I am same caste, same native place, as you? I am not worthy of even kissing you." Suddenly he smiled, a humorless parting of the lips. "But I know what I must say," he added with due deliberation. "I am *sorry*."

She felt herself relax. "It's all right," she said. "I understand."

"Do you?" His reaction was instantaneous. "That is truly wonderful, Sandy. Because I, I am not understanding anything."

She looked at him, heard the bitterness in his voice, and knew she must walk away. But she also saw the pale features of Chippie, the wispy beard, the incipient paunch, the soft unexercised flesh, and wondered what it might be like to be made love to by the hard body of this son of the soil. This is crazy, Sandy, she said to herself. What do you think you're doing here, where you don't belong?

"Come on, Shantan," she said quietly. "It's time we got back to the house."

He nodded, and stepped forward. He was closer to her now

than when she had held his hand. "I was only wanting," he said hoarsely, "to know what it was like."

He smiled sadly at her, and she was suffused with an ineffable sorrow at the unbridgeable chasm between them. In the depths of her pity for his hopeless yearning, she realized both that he would not try to kiss her again, and that she would not resist him if he did.

Neither of them spoke a word. When they had smoothed their clothes back into place and begun to walk back to the house in silence, it was dark. Sandy could no longer see the face of the youth who had sought admission to her world, and to her body. She wished she had the language to enter his thoughts.

They reached the verandah of the main house. In a few steps they would be at the doorway of the living room, and it would be too late to say anything. She could not leave everything unsaid. She touched his arm and, in a voice that was little more than a whisper, spoke the only words that occurred to her.

"Thank you, Shantan," she said. But of course he would never understand why she said it.

1972

The Temple Thief

The flashlight beam danced along the temple walls, casting an uncertain yellow penumbra on the irregular surface.

The light was growing fainter now; Raghav had been unable to afford a new set of batteries, and the light flickered as it traversed another empty niche and came to settle on the last movable idol, a stony, graven image of Shiva sitting impassively in a corner.

Raghav felt the sweat on his palm making his grip on the torch clammy and passed it from one hand to the other. Then he walked forward, towards the statue.

Despite himself, Raghav could not totally prevent a small shudder passing through him as he neared the idol. The fact that he was going to pick it up in a moment and deposit it with its fellows in the large gunny sack he had left on the floor behind him did not rob it of its essentially awesome quality. There was something ominous about the statue's unblinking repose; something fearsomely self-contained, as if the idol was assured of its eventual triumph over all forces of evil, from atheists to temple thieves.

Not that Raghav was, or ever had been, an atheist; religion had been in his bloodstream ever since he could remember. But crime was an economic necessity and one could not let one's scruples, religious or otherwise, interfere with one's necessities. If God could not fill his belly by divine action, Raghav was surely justified in using God to fill his purse—and his belly—by actions which if nothing else had a context of divinity.

And being a temple thief was so much better, and safer, than being a pickpocket or a blind-alley rapist. It was in many ways a respectable line; stealing from the exponents of religion to sell to the connoisseurs of art.

Once more, Raghav studied the statue, trying to ignore the little clutch of fear that stabbed at his heart as he contemplated its fate.

For an irrational moment he wondered whether he needed to take it at all. The temple had been stripped bare already; his sack was almost full. Would one more statue make that much of a difference?

But as he asked himself the question he knew what his own answer would be. In his profession he could not afford to be finicky.

He laid his hands on the Shiva.

The strange, unmoving countenance stared back at him, he felt mockingly. Do you really think you are going to get away with this? It seemed to ask. Do you really believe that you, a mere mortal, and a common thief at that, can capture me?

The little knot of fear in his chest tightened suddenly and the flashlight went out. Cursing, he banged it against his palm, and the light shone straight into Shiva's face. Startled, Raghav almost dropped the flashlight.

I'm getting weak, he snarled at himself, wiping his brow. This is no way to behave. Steeling his nerve, he stuffed the flashlight into a pocket and reached out for the Shiva in the dark with both his hands. It had settled well into its corner and he had to wrench it out of its place. Finally, it came away in his hands, and grunting, he walked back to the sack with it.

It was not as heavy as he thought it might be. He could still sling the sack over his shoulder and make his way out of the temple, across the moonlit track, away from the village and onto the road—and safety.

But he did not. Something held him back—a last forgotten vestige of all that he had held dear and precious. Having committed his crime, he could not leave his place of worship like that. There was a need for some last gesture—a plea for atonement, a kind of expiation. God would understand, God would forgive. Shiva was all-knowing, all-powerful, all-wise. He would not punish a faithful devotee for wanting to keep his bread buttered.

In the darkness, Raghav turned to the center of the temple. He switched the flashlight on and gazed for a long moment at the object behind the railings, an object he had not touched only because it had little market value.

The *lingam*, strong, potent, indestructible, stood there, a symbol of the immutability of the Saivite ethos.

Raghav bent, placing the flashlight on the floor, its light on so he would not lose it, and prostrated himself before his God.

He felt the presence near him before he actually heard any footstep.

Gingerly, he raised his head. The sound of light breathing convinced him his companion was no extra-terrestrial apparition, but an all-too-human intruder.

He was well and truly caught.

A mood of religious obeisance is not the most conducive feeling for resistance. Quietly, overwhelmed by his own guilt, Raghav picked up the flashlight and turned to stare at the face above him.

It was that of a Brahmin priest, attired still in his white *mundu* and wearing the sacred thread, a cotton cloth swathed around his bare chest. Beneath the caste mark on his forehead his deep eyes were kindly, almost indulgent. A small smile played on his ascetic face.

"Rise, my son," the Brahmin said, and his voice was gentle,

deep, and resonant, yet inspiring an instinctively holy awe. Raghav stood, unsteadily, overcome by remorse. The message of the Shiva face had been driven home to him. Evil would always be punished. He would now receive his just retribution.

"I see you are sorry," the priest said quietly. It was almost as if he could read Raghav's mind. "Why did you do this, my son?" The powerful eyes searched his face and Raghav stirred, slightly, but could not speak.

"I think I know," the Brahmin said, and there was a universe of understanding in those words. "Suffering drives men to many things, my son. But . . . this?" There was a genuine sorrow in his voice, mingling with disbelief that Raghav could have stooped so low as to defile that which was sacred to him. In the face of that look, Raghav's eyes fell to the floor. How could he account for his unspeakable crime with facile, hypocritical justifications?

The Brahmin took his arm, gently removing the flashlight from his grasp. He shone it on the sack. "And there lies the result of your depravity," he said, but while the words were strong, the voice spoke more in sorrow than in anger. "You were praying when I came upon you. Do you believe you deserve to be forgiven for this crime?"

Raghav stuttered a reply. His shame was writ large over his face. "No . . . I—am . . . sorry."

"Sorrow is easily expressed, my son," the priest rejoined. "In our religion there is much we tolerate—much the Lord tolerates. It is written that he who does not have must strive to attain success." He looked sharply at the crestfallen Raghav. "But at the expense of others—and not just of one person, but of the entire community which maintains, in its worship, this temple and all within it—that is a cardinal sin."

Raghav did not know what to say as this fresh reminder of the magnitude of his guilt struck him.

"And yet," the Brahmin's voice resumed its gentle, priestly tone, "there is no sin so great that the Lord in his goodness cannot forgive. Provided the sinner acknowledges his sin; provided he admits of the nature of his misdeeds, the Lord accepts his pleas for forgiveness, and enjoins upon him a future adherence to the path of virtue. You, my son, have chosen to prostitute your religion to the deity of wealth—to rob your own temple of an idol that will, perchance, be made to cross the seas to form part of the heretic collection of some beef-eating American nonbeliever." He looked pointedly at Raghav again and the hapless thief trembled in his guilt. "And yet—and yet you are not beyond redemption. For in that moment of prayer, I knew that you were not totally lost to the worship of an alien Mammon. I knew you could be saved."

He stopped and placed his gaze upon Raghav, one arm still on his shoulder, eyes penetrating into the inner recesses of Raghav's dark soul. "You must change your ways, my son. Let not this encounter with the mighty power of the Lord be totally without effect. You are not an irreligious man. You can yet grow in the service of the Lord. Abandon your sinful ways, my son, leave the path of dishonesty and vice and return to the way of righteousness. Leave now—but never again turn to this means of living. And may the Lord go with you."

It was a dismissal—an unbelievably warmhearted one.

Raghav's eyes widened as he looked up at the Man of God. Here was an example of the magnanimity of the Lord! He was being forgiven, set free, given another chance to relive his life. He would use his freedom now to mend the twisted patterns of his existence. His face lifted, and in his relief, an entire new world of hope and promise opened up before him.

He looked at the Brahmin with dumb gratitude.

There was nothing he could say; there was too much to be said. Tears sprang into his eyes as he clasped the priest's hands and sank to his knees to kiss his benefactor's feet.

Then, his tears streaming down his cheeks, he stumbled mutely past the stuffed sack, out of the temple. The Brahmin smiled sagely at his retreating back.

For a long moment, the criminal's flashlight still in his hand, the Brahmin stood thus, smiling his wisdom. Idly he allowed the faint beam to splash over the almost overflowing sack on the floor. Then, slowly, deliberately, he sighed. Switching the flashlight off, he padded soundlessly to where the sack lay and picked it up, feeling its weight in his hands. Then, with his smile no longer on his face, he walked to the temple doorway. For a full minute he stood still, his watchful eyes traveling in every direction, his ears pricked for the slightest sound. Then he heaved the sack over his shoulder, cast a last surreptitious look around him for pursuers, and disappeared into the night.

1971

The Simple Man

"Have you ever received a letter from someone who is dead?" the man at the bar asked, of no one in particular.

A few faces, mildly interested, turned towards him. He had been drinking a great deal; his eyes were bloodshot, his speech slurred, his grip on his glass unsteady. He sat slouched on the tall bar stool, his body crumpled, dependent totally on the bar rail for support.

"No, never had the mortification," someone said. "Why—have you?"

"Yes." The man did not even look at his questioner, but perhaps that was simply because he was in too advanced a state of inebriation. "I have—today. This evening a letter arrived, postmarked Ludhiana, from my friend Karan Dhillon. Karan was then dead exactly five minutes. Only, he'd been here in Trivandrum for a week."

"Oh." The questioner sounded disappointed, for the explanation did not sound extraordinary at all. He had hoped for an alcoholic tall tale. "Well, what with the rail strike and the way the mails are being delayed, your friend may well have posted the letter before he left for Trivandrum—eight or nine days for a letter is hardly unusual at this time."

"Yes," said the man at the bar dully. "Yes . . . indeed, that's exactly what did happen." He still stared ahead, in a world of his own, making no further move to communicate.

His embryonic audience began to lose interest in him. What had promised to be an intriguing story looked as though it was degenerating into just another dipsomaniac rambling. He had almost been forgotten when another fellow—a young, nervous-looking individual sitting across from him—plucked up his courage and asked:

"Karan Dhillon? You mean the cricketer?"

The man tried to locate the new voice, but his eyes couldn't focus with ease. "I mean the cricketer."

"Plays for Punjab?"

"Played for Punjab." There was the ghost of a smile, a strangely bitter wisp of amusement at his own punctilious emphasis. Never could tolerate solecisms, even if drunk.

"Oh, my God." The cricket fan seemed genuinely upset. His voice sounded hollow, empty, as though the loss had been personal. "He was a friend of yours?"

"Yes," the man at the bar said. "Yes, he was a friend of mine . . . the closest friend I've ever had." He seemed to relapse consciously into silence, his mind elsewhere, at an anonymous plot in a cemetery perhaps. The air in the barroom was thick with silence. It was the man himself who broke it, speaking in a strange, distant, almost disembodied voice.

"We grew up together, walked and played and fought together, worked and studied and holidayed together, loved and lost together, cried and laughed together, learned to face the world together. . . . We went to the same public school in Dehra Dun, graduated from the same college in Delhi . . . and then we parted, me to return to Trivandrum as a Government officer, he to Punjab to continue the family tradition of absentee landlordism . . . but distances never kept us apart. He came and visited me here, four, five, six times, and I've lost count of how often I've been to Ludhiana at every conceivable opportunity . . . Oh yes, we were friends, Karan and I. Friends—to the death."

His voice trailed off into the now familiar silence. No one in the room trusted himself to break it. There was something intensely personal and moving in the man's loss, and the pathos of his suffering seemed to come from deep inside that dispirited body. Shattered and desolate, he sank his head on to his outstretched arm, ignoring the drink at the end of it. His friend's death seemed to have affected him far too deeply for a decent man to probe him about it. But it had seemed as though he wanted to talk, to get it out of his system.

The cricket fan, for one, seemed unwilling to let the matter rest at that. He had idolized Karan Dhillon, though he had never seen him; but he had read so much about the swashbuckling "gentleman cricketer" of Punjab who had captured the imagination of sportscribes with his aggressive and stylish strokeplay, yet had never been looked upon favorably by the national-team selectors. Karan Dhillon, the tempestuous enigma, a man who could produce sixes at will and yet fall so often to incredibly poor shots, a cricketer who, in his element, could bowl out any batting side in the country and yet was often made to look worse than pedestrian. Karan Dhillon who went through all his matches with an expressionless poker face and shunned the photographers who wanted to immortalize it. "What kind of a man was Karan Dhillon?" the cricket fan asked, breathlessly.

Slowly, almost painfully, the man at the bar stool righted himself, and smiled sardonically again. "A very simple man," he said at length, "a very simple man indeed. Quite at variance with his public image. Nothing Karan did on the field was really indicative of the stormy, proud nature sportswriters kept foisting on him. Karan played cricket that way because that was the only way he knew how to play it. He revealed no emotion in public, primarily because he didn't see the need to. You see, Karan Dhillon was a man of very simple likes and dislikes. He did only what he wanted to do and then did it to the best of his ability. He took avidly to any sport because physical activity suited him and he had a keen eye and quick reflexes. Both in school and college he played for the team in four or five games, captaining both Doon and St. Stephen's at cricket—no mean feat, I assure you. Naturally—or characteristically—what he was good at became his primary interest as well. He spent almost all his time playing one game or the other, depending on the weather. At his air-conditioned bungalow on the outskirts of Ludhiana he possessed what was probably the only radio this side of the Suez Canal that caught the BBC internal sports broadcasts. That's how much of a sports fanatic he was."

The man paused in his narrative to take a long gulp from his glass before resuming again. "Karan was a very easy person to get along with. All that he was intensely concerned about was sports, especially cricket, an easygoing life, and the well-being of his six-foot-two-inch, two-hundred pound muscular frame. Very simple concerns. Little else upset him. Karan knew no other philosophy, and this one suited him well. There were very few things he did want, and what he wanted he easily got with his family's money. This meant there was little he was desperate about. It is very difficult to come into conflict with a man like that."

The man gulped down the rest of his drink and called for another. Beads of perspiration stood out on his forehead, and his eyes were beginning to bulge. "Karan, however, made few real friends. Despite the fact that as a sports hero he was fairly well-known, he tended to keep out of the mainstream of college life because he didn't see what he had to gain by 'smiling and saying hello to every toady who passes me' as he put it. Because of his singular lack of ambition and his disinclination to exert himself to further his own interests, I found it very easy to get along with him. And I shared some of his interests, such as an amateur penchant for sports criticism, so that made things much easier. He was a very simple man, direct and straightforward, and ours was a very simple relationship—the deep friendship of two men who accepted each other for what we were worth and learned to admire and respect our individual attributes. In a way, I suppose, I tended to dominate the relationship, for I was bright and brilliant and ambitious and extroverted while Karan, who was none of these things, proved only too willing to let me force myself on him. He usually didn't mind; but when he did he showed it, and when he showed it he usually got his own way."

The fresh drink had now arrived, and the man took a long draught. Miraculously, he was still speaking coherently. He must have had a whole vat inside him, thought the cricket fan, and the way his eyes were struggling to maintain clear sight it was evident that his line of vision was as crooked as a chucker's bowling arm. Pupils bleary, he resumed, doggedly maintaining clarity in both speech and thought process.

"It was a comfortable relationship, and we both enjoyed it. As I said before, Karan was a very simple man, and it was his very simplicity that marked the keynote of our friendship. Because he kept it on a simple level, it remained all these years, uncomplicated by the tensions that tend to creep in to any alliance of disparate forces." He took another sip and lost the trend of his conversation. "He would drop in often to my office and pull my leg about my secretary, a buxom, matronly forty-year-old with glasses whom he called '7.5' on account of her lens power. 'Still busy chasing 7.5 round the desk, eh?' he would often ask when he met me. I mean, that was the kind of chap he was—even his humor stayed on that simple, earthy plane.

"I called him 'Punjabi'—really, that was the most egregious thing about him, his Punjabiness, and he retaliated with a lot of 'Southey' jokes of dubious taste and quality. But our ribbing of each other was always good-natured, the ethnic conflict could scarcely exist with our cosmopolitan backgrounds and the 'Punjabi' and the 'Southey' remained simple jokes that were an integral part of our very simple relationship. . . ." The man reached into an inside-pocket and pulled out a sheet of paper. "This will show you what I mean—his last letter: the one which arrived today. . . ."

He held it out; the cricket fan took it from him eagerly, and a couple of necks craned over his shoulder as the young fellow read it out in a quavering voice.

Hey P.M.:—Too busy running after 7.5 to drop me a line as promised? Or maybe it's the Ludhiana postal service, but anyway do write soon and confirm, since I've got to make my booking well in advance (waiting for two weeks at Indian Airlines). Looking forward to seeing you in Southieland again. . . . Did you see the Davis Cup? It seemed that the quantity of games rather than their quality provided all the excitement. How did Southey No. 2 play so well? All the Southey cricketers in England are in bad form—missing their spicy breakfasts? Wadekar's going great, and Solkar's a fantastic chap. Two new young guys—Madan Lal and Patel—almost certain for First Test. The Bengal Prodigy has *phailed* badly, and your favorite commentator Rajan Bala is trying to make all sorts of excuses for him (read *H. Standard* of 14th? I've sent a critical letter, though it may be too strong for them to print). . . . So what have you been up to? (Besides chasing 7.5 and hatching government plots.) I have been playing some tennis and golf, and promptly ended up with a backache (like Wadekar had last evening vs. Worcestershire.) It has been rather hot, but fortunately not too many power outages. The one day I spent in Cal last month, there was load-shedding from 9 to 1 (morning) and 9 to 2 (night): Thank God this is Punjab, not Bengal. Any news of Surdy as yet? Lob the ball back into court soon—Punjabi.

The cricket fan, having concluded his locution, folded the missive reverently and handed it back. The man at the bar pocketed it carefully.

"That was typical of him—all his letters were like that. Whenever he thought of me he dashed off a line. This time he didn't wait for the vagaries of the railwaymen to subside and my 'confirmation.' He came down on the earliest available flight—I was unfortunately away on an official trip to the district."

The man's breath was coming faster now, and he was speaking in jerks. His face was totally bathed in sweat. "When he came to Trivandrum, I wasn't at home," he uttered hoarsely, taking a large gulp. "I wasn't at home."

A strange look came over his face. "You should have met my wife. A Bengali girl. Mamta. I've always liked Bengalis, and I love Mamta. Wonderful name, isn't it? Mamta—love and yet not just love, something more, something higher. . . . There was always that 'something more' in our relationship, just as there was 'something more' in Mamta that set her apart from other girls. . . . Ours was, of course, what they call a love marriage. The first time I met her I thought she was a bitch; we argued bitterly over something inconsequential and parted, each vowing never to speak to the other again. . . . Of course neither kept that vow. She was beautiful, that woman—exquisite—and she was mine. . . ." He took a quick swallow. "I remember thinking she came as near to perfection in a woman as I've sought . . . the only blemishes I could discern in her were the imperfectly cured acne of late adolescence and a slight affectation in attitude . . . but those were minor blemishes. I loved her, and she reciprocated. We were married—this time . . . last year. Tomorrow to the day." He drained his glass again. "I loved my Mamta. She appealed to everything that was weak in me, but I loved her. She was the only woman capable of arousing in me the emotions of possessiveness, of jealousy, of brute, animal passion. I worshipped the very ground she walked on—at least when she wasn't looking." He gave a dry, bibulous laugh, but his face still carried that look of intense emotion, and the words seemed to be wrung out of some bloody laceration in his heart. He was not drinking now. "I am a fairly cool person in my everyday dealings, but no one could understand how much Mamta meant to me—how for me, she was my everything, without whom life would have no meaning . . . at all. . . .

"Karan never understood. I suppose that was his basic defect; with all his simplicity and candor he was incapable of appreciating that I, of all people, could have an even more significant relationship on a deeper level with my wife. He never understood that." His face was contorted now. In the still, stifling atmosphere of the barroom, no one so much as breathed.

"I came back from my official trip this evening at 4:30, by car. . . . I let myself in with my key, opened the front door, and stepped into the corridor. Then I saw them . . . they hadn't even bothered to shut the bedroom door. Mamta never could resist he-men. . . . They heard me, and turned in shock—I will never forget the look on their faces. Somehow it was not merely the infidelity that blew my mind, but the fact that it was Karan— with my Mamta . . . ! In that second, something snapped. I scarcely remember what happened next. There was a ceremonial dagger hanging on the corridor wall as a kind of decoration . . . before I knew what I was doing it was over. I don't know how often I stabbed them both. . . . I just lashed out at their defenseless, naked bodies till there was no strength left in my arm— then I just stood and saw with horror what I had done. I stumbled to the bathroom. There was blood all over me. . . . I had barely begun washing myself when the bell rang. I froze in terror. Who could it be? The police? A visitor? Some neighbor who had heard the noise—had there been noise? I was too frightened to think. But I had to open that door. I whipped off my bloodstained clothes, quickly washed the blood from my face. . . . The bell rang again. I hurriedly tied a towel around my waist and opened the door in a dead fright. It was the postman. . . . I could have swooned with relief. I accepted the letter, thanked him with a demented grin, and slammed the door—it was only then that I saw the envelope, recognized the handwriting on the cover. Then I broke down. . . ."

His eyes swam in tears as he relived the experience, and finally the dam burst, the rivulets of salty sorrow came cascading down his cheeks, and he buried his face in his hands, sobbing huge, racking tears as his chest heaved on the bar rail. . . .

The cricket fan was wide-eyed in horror. Meanwhile, a large man who had been sitting next to him got up, went over to the man at the bar, put a protective arm around him, and said, "Come on, Southey. You've got it out of your system. You can go home now." The man sobbed.

"What do you mean?" The cricket fan was on his feet. "You can't simply let him go like that—he's a criminal! A murderer! He's confessed—we should call the police!"

The large man looked at him patiently, like a kindergarten teacher attempting to explain to a particularly belligerent kid that he cannot speak until he raises one finger. "I see you're new here. This is a pretty frequent occurrence, I'm told—ask the bartender. Poor Southey—unsuccessful novelist, failed sportsman, marital dropout: the murder is a recurring fantasy. And this is the only way he can get rid of it—by working the frustrations out of himself."

The cricket fan didn't know whether he was disappointed or surprised. "And Mamta? What about Mamta?" he asked.

"She doesn't exist—she never existed, I'm afraid. She was the main character of his first short story—rejected by forty-seven magazines at home and abroad. He still hasn't got over it—but he will, poor chap. As long as I'm here, I'll see he does."

"But how do you know all this?" the cricket fan was bewildered. "Who are you?"

"Oh—yes, I suppose I should have introduced myself," said the large man with the strangely impassive face, unblinkingly. "I'm Karan Dhillon."

1974

The Professor's Daughter

The only remarkable thing about old Chhatwal was his daughter.

"Old Chhatwal," we all called him, though no one really knew exactly how old Professor Chhatwal was. He had been at college ever since anybody could remember—and some memories, especially those of the khaki uniformed mess bearers, went back a long way. As far as anyone knew, old Chhatwal had been planted on the premises along with the foundation stone. Generations of students recalled the same placid face, the wispy, perpetually greying beard that needed neither wax nor net, the immaculate cotton turban in its invariable shade of dark maroon. It seemed he had always looked like that; his students aged in the world outside, but Professor Chhatwal, content in the cocoon of college, remained eternal, as immutable and unchanging as his philosophy lectures.

Philosophy was not a subject in great demand those days, but Chhatwal's standing owed little to his skills as a teacher. His lecture notes, it was said, had not been updated since the Second World War, and he read aloud from them at dictation speed, looking up from the yellowing sheets in his hand only to check that the time honored words were indeed being taken down. If anyone was naive, or optimistic, enough to ask a question, Professor Chhatwal's standard reply was, "I will come to that later." Sometimes, by ploughing relentlessly on through his changeless text, he did; more often, unless the question was particularly elementary, he did not, and the inquirer learned to take his curiosity to the library, to a senior student, or to another tutor. Most of us acquired old Chhatwal's wisdom secondhand through notes handed down by our predecessors and went to his classes only to fulfill the minimum attendance requirements for the university exam. On these occasions we usually tried to catch up with our correspondence home, taking care to look up periodically from our writing in order to ensure that our diligence was noted by an appreciative Professor. Frequently, though, we slipped out of class as soon as the roll had been called and our presence registered. In the senior years this habit was so rampant that on one occasion, or so popular legend had it, old Chhatwal paused in his reading to find every seat in the classroom vacant.

Nor did Professor Chhatwal adopt a more exciting persona outside the confines of his lectures. He never sought conversation, and when it was imposed upon him, replied in the same quiet, measured tones that so effectively put his students to sleep at their desks. Some collegians, infected by the popular tendency to award nicknames to their betters, tried irreverently to dub him Chatty. But even the unsubtle irony of this contraction of the Professor's name did not guarantee its wide acceptance, for Chhatwal was acknowledged to lack the minimal qualities required to merit even behind-the-back familiarity. It was impossible to arouse him to any kind of animation. There were teachers who, though duds at the blackboard, came to life after hours as Staff Advisers to the Drama Society or the Mountaineering Club, but old Chatty was not among them. Amid the excitement and activity of campus life, Chatty remained serenely unmoved by the energies and passions expended around him. There was a rumor that he had once offered himself as the faculty adviser for a Lepidopterists' Society, but had not found enough students willing to join one. Though since no one had ever spotted old Chatwal with a butterfly net—nor, indeed, seen him taking any interest in any other of nature's creations, winged or otherwise—the rumor was generally discounted.

And yet Professor Chhatwal was an institution at college. He may only, it was true, have become one by sheer survival, but he was one for all that. He required no outstanding academic achievement, no extraordinary personal characteristic, to affirm his standing. His very presence had made him a frame of reference, a sign of stability, a reassurance that the college's traditions continued unimpaired. When one of us met an Old Boy at a social gathering or at a job interview, one of the first questions we were sure to be asked was "and how's old Chatty?" The college's most distinguished alumni were, almost axiomatically, its oldest ones, and the only professor surviving from their days was the durable Chhatwal; so he correspondingly gained in eminence from being recalled by the eminent. This was reinforced with very little effort on his part: any former student, returning to the campus for a visit and shaking his head over how much had changed for the worse in three (or fifteen, or thirty-five) years, had only to see Professor Chhatwal taking his leisurely constitutional near the Chapel to console himself that some things, at least, were as he remembered.

Three times a day Professor Chhatwal walked through the college campus: twice to and from classes, and once, in the early evening, for what might, had he revealed more energy, been called exercise. On these occasions he was usually accompanied by his wife, a *salwar-kameez*-clad matron of indeterminate shape, who waddled determinedly by his side, face set with the effort, steel bangles clinking as she pumped her short arms. Past the dining hall they went, old Chhatwal like lethargy on legs, his wife a curiously ineffective dynamo, across the rose garden, round the Chapel, once, twice, along the library and finally down the dusty path to their campus home. It was an unvarying routine for the professor, and a frequent one for his spouse, but it seemed to make little difference to old Chatty whether he was accompanied or not. In all the years and all the evenings that the two of them took their evening walk together, no one ever saw the Chhatwals exchange a single word.

The Chhatwal constitutional thus passed into the routine of college, like the gong after classes or the unchanging fare at the mess. The walk was as unremarkable in its regularity as everything else about the old professor. Had he failed to emerge one day, or changed his route, it would have been noticed, but he did not, and the rule about old Chhatwal remained that there was never anything worth noticing about him.

And then one day his daughter joined him in his walk.

She must have been in her midteens that first time: fifteen, sixteen perhaps, certainly a year or two younger than the youngest student at college. Some of the boys were dimly aware that Chhatwal had a child, but few had any idea of its age or gender. The child undoubtedly played in her own back-yard, went to school, and did whatever else it was little children did, but her existence had not impinged on the consciousness of the college. Even those who visited the Chhatwal home for tutorials, or in fulfillment of other unavoidable obligations, had never seen her. The impact made by her emergence was therefore little short of seismic.

I was in my room, at my desk, plagiarizing a tutorial I had received at third remove from a long-departed senior, when Bunny burst in, eyes wild with excitement. "Come and look! You won't believe this! Come and look!"

"Forget it, Bunny," I replied in scholastic indolence. "Can't you see I'm working?"

"Just come and see what Chhatwal's walking around with," he urged, and ran back to the balcony.

I sighed, rose, and walked to the edge of the brick veranda to see what the fuss was all about. The first thing I noticed was that about fifty other students, and not all freshers either, had the same idea. The verandas and windows of the surrounding dormitory blocks, usually curtained or shuttered against the afternoon heat, were overflowing with adolescent curiosity. The object of their attention strolled obliviously beneath on the path that skirted our lawn.

The Chhatwal family was out in strength. By the professor's side various lumps and layers of matronly flesh swayed and wobbled in arhythmic discordance as Mrs. Chhatwal labored under a too-tight *salwar-kameez*. By *her* side walked a slim, fine-featured girl, pale face cheerful in repose, lissome limbs draped in a plain *salwar-kameez* that seemed to have been made in a different world from her mother's. The fading sun of early evening cast changing patterns of light and shadow on her face, her dress, her bare forearms, her creamy feet in dark Kolhapuri *chappals*. We stared transfixed as the procession ambled out of our line of vision. For once Professor Chhatwal's stately pace seemed too hurried to us.

When at last they had gone, fifty voices simultaneously exhaled their astonishment.

"What a chick, *yaar*!" breathed Bunny.

"Come on, Bunny, she's just a kid," I responded.

"Enough of a woman for me," squeaked Chhotu, the shortest of our group, who had pulled a chair to his window to facilitate his examination of the spectacle.

"Who'd have thought old Chhatwal *capable* of producing goods like that?" marveled Hafiz.

That was certainly part of her allure, of course: the incongruity of her parenthood. That, and the fact that she was the only female of any sort between fifteen and forty within the bounds of college. Not only were we an exclusively all-male institution, but there was not so much as a cleaning-woman allowed on the premises, and the dormitory rooms were barred to visitors of the Prime Minister's sex. The only professors senior enough to be entitled to family housing on the campus were too venerable to have wives worthy of venery, and the only daughter any of them had managed to produce had married and left long before the oldest of my inherited tutorials was written. Little Miss Chhatwal was unique, *sui generis*, one of a kind. She instantly became a college obsession.

Fellows fell over themselves to find out about her. Studies, letters, even games of bridge were abandoned as she walked by. The more adventurous went for walks themselves, respectfully hailing Professor Chhatwal in the hope of being introduced to his offspring, but he invariably acknowledged their greetings with an uncommunicative nod. Whenever he scheduled a tutorial at his house, attendance shot up, though his daughter never so much as walked past his study. If Chhatwal noticed his sudden increase in popularity, he gave no sign of it. He plodded on, while his daughter, and her fame, grew.

Occasionally, a detail slipped out, and this was seized upon by a hundred eager hands and avidly devoured. The younger Chhatwal's name, someone discovered—through a stray reference by her father, or a glimpse of a schoolbook on a shelf—was Jasvinder Kaur. "What a name for a girl like that," Chhotu bleated. "You bloody Surdies name your women as if you were baptising battle tanks." By almost universal consent, the appalling appellation was transmuted to Jazzy. I suppose it says something about college that we all considered this far more suitable.

Jazzy did not accompany her parents on their perambulations every day. Frenzied speculation about her absence centered on the demands of homework, though some darkly declared she was just trying to drive them crazy. When she did come along she was as silent and reserved as the rest of the trio. There was no girlish skip or jump in her stride. She walked straight, in even, measured steps, looking at the path in front of her. Never did her eyes stray to take in her onlooking admirers. But each passing month only enhanced her desirability. The colder season brought a flush to her cheeks; her body seemed to be filling out under her sweater. Even I, formerly so dismissive, soon had to acknowledge she was becoming a woman.

But I don't mean to imply she was some sort of Venus. She didn't have to be, to merit our attention. Any "halfway decent chick," as Bunny put it, would, in that unique position, have done. Jasvinder Kaur Chhatwal was certainly more than halfway decent. The obsession with her therefore grew, unfettered by any sense of proportion.

"Jazzy" became a new code word for the ultimate in female pulchritude and unattainability. To say of the latest new starlet on the Hindi screen that "she's in the Jazzy class, *yaar*" was the highest compliment a collegian could pay. The term was soon extended to mean anything admirable or pleasing—the phrase "that's jazzy" marked its speaker's academic affiliations to our college, at a time when the rest of the university was pathetically content with "freaked out" and even the hoary "groovy." But we were not entirely without a sense of self-mockery: someone dubbed the most efficient waiter in the college mess Jazzy too, and the label stuck.

The Jazzy legend grew, unnourished by any contact with its subject. For two years after what had been dubbed her "coming out" walk no one at college had so much as spoken to her in person, yet her nickname was on every student's lips. A passionate interest in Jazzy was something every freshman acquired to prove he was a full-fledged collegian, along with the received prejudices against the Dean and the secret of the unlatched gate through which curfew-breakers could leave and enter campus after 11 p.m. The myth acquired anecdotal accretions, almost all apocryphal. One student had bribed a *dhobi* to have a whiff of her unwashed laundry. Another had broken into Chhatwal's house and stolen a bra, only to be informed by the worldly-wise that it was certainly

Mrs. Chhatwal's. A third had clambered up on the roof and looked through the skylight while Jazzy bathed. The stories were always secondhand, always about someone else. Whenever names were attached to any of them, it was always of someone who was no longer around to confirm the story.

Inevitably with seventeen to twenty-two-year-olds in our cloistered circumstances, the interest in Jazzy took on explicitly prurient overtones. The rooftop admirer had allegedly discerned a mole on Jazzy's left buttock. This item of received wisdom was passed on with a knowing leer, as if all who alluded to it had verified the mark with their own eyes. If someone wore an exceptionally immaculate white shirt, it was described as being "as spotless as Jazzy's right butt." And so on. Freshers being "ragged" were asked to devise the most original ploys for gaining access to the fabled Jazzy. The exercise facilitated their acculturation at college, but none of their ideas were any good. Most proposed knocking on the door and pretending to be a census officer or health inspector (the twit who suggested "gynecologist" was soundly cuffed but grudgingly admired).

During my final year I decided to apply for admission to American graduate schools. When I told Chhatwal I needed a reference from him, I was not entirely surprised to discover he had never been asked for one before. He looked helplessly at the forms he had to complete, then asked me to bring them to his house after lunch to discuss how he should fill them out.

I must admit that despite my preoccupation with my own future I was far from unaware that I would be entering Jazzy's territory. Not that Bunny and Chhotu would have let me forget it. "Ask him to recommend you to his daughter instead, *yaar*," Chhotu suggested. Hafiz ostentatiously lent me a bottle of eau-de-cologne as I prepared to set out for my appointment.

I felt the heat haze drying up my nervous perspiration as I walked to Chhatwal's house. But when I rang the bell my sweat broke out cold on my palms again. For it was Jazzy who opened the door.

She looked at me expressionlessly. "Come in," she said. Her voice was undistinguished, slightly hoarse.

I nodded gratefully, finding no words, and followed her indoors. It was dark and cool in the front room. The blinds were down to keep out the sun. "I'll go tell my father," she announced, and without waiting for confirmation, turned and walked away from me. I watched her long plait swing behind her, in time with the swaying of her hips. Her hair was not the only thing that had grown since I first set eyes on her more than two years earlier.

"He's just finishing his lunch," she informed me a minute later. "He asked you to wait in the study." Again I could do no more than nod my acquiescence, but with a hesitant movement of her hand she was already leading the way down the corridor.

"This way." The voice was decidedly unremarkable. I thought of the couplets my friends had composed to a voice they had never heard. "Like moonlight made audible," Bunny had extravagantly recited. Not even twilight, *yaar*, I would tell him.

As she ushered me into the sunlit, bookless room that Chhatwal called a study, I took my first good look at her. She was eighteen, long-limbed, full-bodied. With the sun behind her back I could make out the outline of her shape under the flower-patterned cotton *kameez*. My pulse quickening, I found my voice. "Er—you are Jasvinder, aren't you?"

She had half-turned to leave the room but stopped at the door, startled. "How—how did you know my name?" she asked.

"Oh, I think your father told me once," I said airily. "Which college do you go to?"

She looked uncertainly around her. "My—my *father* told you?" she asked, her voice even hoarser.

I began regretting the lie, but I couldn't change my tune now.

"Yes, he has often mentioned you," I plunged in recklessly. "I'm Har Bhajan Singh. Everyone calls me H.B."

"I'd better not call you anything," she said. "My parents won't like it." Her eyes darted nervously down the corridor. "I'm not supposed to talk to you."

"But you just let me in," I pointed out reasonably.

"Only because my mother is ill," she said. "Please—I must go now."

"Don't worry, it'll be all right," I said, very much the older male now. "I'll tell your father." I had not sat down; now I moved closer to her. "Relax," I added, looking directly into her eyes in an effort to still them, to hold the dark pupils in place.

She tensed at my approach, her knuckles tightening on the door handle. "I—I don't know," she said in that small voice, a voice afraid of being used.

"Hey, it's no big deal, you know," I smiled. "I just want to have a little chat while we wait for your Dad, that's all."

She looked at me then, not moving her face, her eyes widening upwards to meet mine. "Papa talked to you about me?" she asked.

"Yes, yes, there's nothing to worry about," I said. "Your father knows me—I've been his student for three years, for God's sake. Relax." I smiled broadly, reassuringly. So it was this frightened mouse about whom such a collection of myths had been built. Wait till I told everyone what she was really like. "Jasvinder—you know what the guys all call you?"

"Me? Why should they call me anything?" She sounded positively alarmed. "I don't know any—guys."

"Sure, but they all know you." I grinned. "Hey, you're a star on campus, Jazzy."

"Jazzy?"

"That's what the guys call you. Jasvinder—Jazzy, see?"

"But—but why? Why? What do I have to do with them?"

"Look, everyone sees you around, you know, walking with your

Dad and Mom, that sort of thing. It's just a little joke, that's all. No one means any harm by it."

"Jazzy." Her voice was strained in a mixture of pain and wonder. "If my father hears of this he'll kill me."

"Don't be silly. Why should he—kill you?" I was beginning to feel uneasy myself. Old Chhatwal, I thought: he wouldn't harm a fly.

"He—he's always told me to keep away from the college boys, to keep to myself. And now you tell me—every boy talks about me?"

"Look, well, not exactly, you know, not talks *about* you, just sort of *mentions* you, if you know what I mean." I placed my hand on hers, on the doorknob, trying to convey reassurance. She froze with an audible intake of breath, her face flushing. Stupidly, in my awkwardness, I froze too, my hand still on hers. Her flush deepened—and turned to reddening panic as a quiet, hard-edged voice cut her fingers away from under mine.

"Jasvinder!"

It was old Chhatwal. He was at the end of the corridor, his body stiff with rage, eyes round with outrage. The girl's freed hand flew to her mouth in dismay.

"Go to your room." He began advancing towards us, his voice still unraised but trembling with the weight of his suppressed fury. The girl backed away from him, her voice almost a whimper. "Papa—but. . . ."

"Go to your room."

"Papa—but—I didn't—he said—you don't underst—"

"Go." The one word was enough. The girl ran stumbling down the corridor, her face in her hands. She may not even have heard him saying, "I shall deal with you later."

"Professor Chhatwal . . ." I had found my voice. "Sir, she—"

"Shut up." He was dangerously near me now, and I saw to my horror that his hands were clenched into throbbing, hairy fists. "Get out of my house, boy."

"But—but I—"

"I don't want to hear another word from you. Get out—unless you want me to throw you out."

I most decidedly did not want him to throw me out. Nor did one tangle with professors in this mood. One of the few lessons I had learned early and learned well was the one about discretion being the better part of valor. I would explain, I decided, later—in a letter.

I futilely waved the recommendation forms at him, then made my way in something of a daze to the door. I heard him shut it quietly behind me, the sound echoing dully in the hollow confusions of my mind.

For a full minute, perhaps longer, I simply stood on the front steps, not knowing what to do and quite incapable of clear thought. Then I heard her voice again, its hoarseness strained by tears. "Papa—please—I didn't. . . ."

A window was open on one side of the house. Impulsively, I ran to it. It was four or five feet above my head. I could not see anything, but the voices carried quite clearly in the still, hot air.

"I want no explanation. You disobeyed me."

"But Papa, he—I—I didn't. . . ."

"I am not interested in your protestations, Jasvinder. If I cannot trust you to open the door for a boy without your becoming intimate with him, I will have failed as a father. And I do not intend to fail." There was a clatter, as if something had been picked up.

"But—Papa—not that, please—not *that* again, please."

"I am sorry; there is only one penalty for disobedience, Jasvinder. You know the punishment."

"Papa—please, I can't take it. . . ."

"Don't waste my time, girl. Bend over."

Suddenly I realized what was happening. In my incredulity I knew it was not enough to hear those words. I had to see.

A few feet away from the side of the house stood a mango tree. Without pausing to think I ran to it and began clambering up. The distinct thwack of wood hitting flesh assailed my ears before my eyes reached the same level as the window. It was followed by a yelp like that of a scalded puppy. I braced myself against the tree trunk, held onto a branch above my head, and looked in.

They were both turned away from me. Jazzy was bent over the side of her bed, her *salwar* pulled down from her hips to bare her rear. Despite my shock I noticed, with the absurd precision of a man in a dream, that there was no mole on the exposed buttocks, left or right.

What there was, though, was an ugly red stripe. And another, as her father, with a swift, strong stroke, brought a wooden ruler crashing down on Jazzy's pathetically pale skin.

From my vantage point Chhatwal's face was in profile. But even at that angle I could see how it was distorted by his anger, how the eyes were puffed up and bloodshot, how the veins stood up on his huge hand as he wielded the ruler in deliberate punition. I was so close he should have seen me, but he was in a world of his own, completely absorbed in a reality circumscribed by his rage, his daughter's behind, and the instrument by which he could inflict the one upon the other.

With each stroke the girl flinched, vainly suppressing a cry. The tears streaming down her cheeks fell on her hands, the hands I had so thoughtlessly held. I stood transfixed, watching in a blur the professor's repeatedly raised arm, the regular rise and fall of the ruler, the shuddering of the girl's body, the mass of red blotches and welts multiplying across the pale posterior. And then the ruler broke. Chhatwal dropped it in a gesture of finality. He turned to leave the room, and as I tumbled from my perch to the ground I noticed that his face had again been restored to its habitual expression of calm complacency.

I did not stop running until I had reached my own dormitory block.

When Hafiz came by for his eau-de-cologne he asked the inevitable question.

"So did you see Jazzy?"

I looked at him for a long moment, revelations, explanations, exaggerations clashing within me for release. And then I saw before me the image of Jasvinder Kaur Chhatwal, bared and beaten, whimpering her pain, pleading to be spared.

"No," I replied. "She wasn't there."

1975

Friends

Sharing the same room, as Camus once wrote, leads to a strange kind of alliance between men. It's as if they fraternize, not just in the waking day, but in the night too, in the "ancient community" of dream and fatigue.

That's the way it was with Vicky and me. We'd shared the same room in the college dormitory for two years, and a special bond had developed between us. It wasn't just that we were always together; what surprised people more was the infinite delight we found in each other's company, even after all that time. We faced life together, or what we understood by "life" at college: cut classes together, went to movies together, acted in plays together, chased girls together. If Vicky wanted a cigarette—as he often did—I would be sure to accompany him to the *dhaba*, even though I didn't smoke. If I felt like a cup of tea, Vicky, who detested the stuff, would come along with me to the café. There was hardly anything about each other we didn't know; hardly any problem we didn't tackle together, any vagary of college life we didn't turn to each other to surmount. The same situations never ever seemed to stale with us, the same jokes never palled, the same company never turned dull. It was as if we were made for each other in a special kind of way that was different from, and in a way above, our other relationships, even with girls.

People often said this kind of friendship was dangerous, that sooner or later it would come to an unhealthy end. But somehow Vicky and I had such a perfect understanding of each other that things never reached a head. He would instinctively know when I wanted to be left alone or to study, and I would somehow sense when he was in one of his moods and didn't want to be disturbed. We turned to each other frequently because we both possessed the same basic outlook on life: mercenary, devil-may-care, self-possessed. We'd have long arguments on things, but both of us were too easygoing to possess ideologies, and the battles often ended in comfortable compromises. We never fought over anything because it was more convenient not to, and somehow, nothing was worth fighting over in any case.

By some miracle, for instance, we never went after the same girl. As soon as one of us displayed interest in a female, the other quietly turned to look for fresh pastures for himself. In any case, girls didn't matter enough for us to quarrel over them. To us, girls were meant for light flirtations, to be occasionally brought up to one's room and given the once-over, to be used when possible to fulfill one's unavoidable biological desires. Our interest was casual enough to be dispassionate, and we'd usually get together and discuss a recent episode in clinical detail. That's all there was to it.

And then one thing that kept us together was our sense of humor—puns were almost our monopoly in the college dormitory and we had something of the reputation of being the local answer to Peter Cook and Dudley Moore. You should meet Vicky sometime. He's the type of person everyone takes an instant liking to: physically small and slight, with a perpetually mock-serious expression on his face, a shock of hair falling over his right eye which he was always unsuccessfully attempting to brush away, a cheerful attitude to people—and a lack of inhibition with his jokes that kept even newcomers in stitches. Vicky was everybody's friend in a way even I couldn't manage to be; I was General Secretary of our College Students' Union, popular but somehow never really one of the guys, while Vicky, who'd campaigned for me and virtually won me the election, had refused a post in my Cabinet so that he could all the more freely criticize me for my shortcomings. You know, that's the kind of guy he was—everyone wanted him around because they felt he would never want anything out of them.

In a way that was perhaps a disadvantage. Since he was so much in demand that he never needed to go out of his way to be nice to people, he often ended up unintentionally hurting them. Some of his jokes were just too pointed, many of his comments directly rude, much of his behavior insensitively casual, and he never made an effort to gauge the mood or the spirit of his audience.

Nor was he a respecter of persons or occasions. But he never suffered for it. Everyone knew he never meant anything seriously, and people easily forgave and forgot his failings.

Till Rekha came.

Rekha was not the usual type of sultry siren you imagine breaking up male friendships. Thin to the point of boniness, tall and short-haired, she was attractive only because of a natural grace that lent bearing to her narrow figure, and a small, remarkably lively face that made every sentence she spoke worth watching in rapt attention. Her expressions were astonishingly mobile; her eyes, a deep black in which you felt you could drown, danced in a way that would have captivated the most jaded nawab. But Vicky and I might never have come close enough to notice any of this, were it not for the fact that she was also one of the most brilliant debaters in the university.

Naturally, I met her at a debate. I had always fancied myself something of a speaker (indeed, with Vicky interjecting from the floor and me declaiming at the mike, there never was an audience shortage at any debate in the university). All the other teams had spoken but us and Lady Wellesley College, and knowing that L.W. was being represented by a fresher team, I was convinced the trophy was ours. Lack of competition always brings out the best in me; I was in my element that day, punning, rebutting, ridiculing the motion. When I stepped off the stage to tumultuous applause, I thought we had won and the first prize was mine. Then Rekha stepped on stage. You should have seen the way the customary buzz of an audience at an uninteresting-looking speaker suddenly stopped the moment she started speaking. That day I learned to give a new meaning to the old cliché about a pin-drop silence, give or take a minor vowel: I dropped a pen and you should have seen the looks I got. She demolished my speech, tore apart Vicky's half-hearted interjection·and triumphantly strode off with the first prize. It was a virtuoso performance, and, coming from a fresher, a totally stunning upset. Chastened, I went up to her and said, "Congrats."

"Thanks," she said. "You were good."

I was about to make some deprecating remark when Vicky strolled up. "I liked your interjection," she said, smiling.

"I can see you did," replied Vicky ruefully.

"By the way, this is Vicky Vohra," I said, completing the introductions.

"VV for short," Vicky said.

"You mean wee-wee," I quickly added, grinning. Rekha laughed.

"Why don't we go somewhere to spend your prize-money?" Vicky asked, grinning.

"I wouldn't mind," she replied, unexpectedly. "Where do you suggest?"

"Oh, we wouldn't dream of depriving you of your hard-earned cash—but PM can *rise* to the occasion with his second-prize *dough*." Vicky puns so often it becomes instinctive, even when he isn't trying to. "How about the college café, PM?" Vicky called me PM (the initials of my name) because he said it stood for the things I sought in life—prize money, perfect mammaries, and (ultimately) the Prime Ministry.

"Fine," I said, and we set out for college, with Rekha walking in the middle. Somehow in any other girl her ready acceptance of our invitation would have been construed as the proof of a "fast" female. But with Rekha it seemed just an indication of her innocent friendliness. And friendly she was; she bubbled over with charm, and to Vicky and me, unaccustomed to a female whose prime asset was not her body, it was an experience just being with her.

"This is Ramlal's *dhabha*," Vicky explained, as we strolled in through the college gate. "He's been in the college campus ever since we moved from Kash Gate."

"Which, as some people unkindly say, is named after him," I added.

"Yes, he does very well, dispensing tea and cigarettes to us unfortunates at a few paise above the market price," Vicky said. "We have to buy from him, though, because it's a hell of a fag trying to get cigarettes elsewhere. And the liquids he sells are pretty *tea*-rible too."

"You mean they're *kaafi* bad?" Rekha asked, mischievously. *Kaafi*, in this context, is Hindi for "rather," as well as for the brown beverage. I grinned my appreciation.

"You're catching on, young lady," Vicky approved, paternally.

We entered the café. For once, heads swiveled around at our entrance—not because we had a girl with us but because that girl was so plain. Our standing as the Casanovas of college took a pretty hard knock that day.

We chose a corner table and waved Rekha to the first seat.

"You've got me cornered, have you?" she asked.

"No, no," I replied, "this way you've got an edge over us."

She laughed—a soft, musical, exceedingly pleasant tinkle. You really felt you had just delivered an epigram that Wilde might have won an Oscar for. It was a laugh that went straight to the head.

"Three chairs for us," Vicky noted, as we sat down. "Hip hip hooray."

The waiter materialized, as our café waiters seem to do only when they see you with a girl. Rekha refused to order anything but a Coke. "I really don't have much at teatime," she said in self-justification.

Vicky, characteristically, was most liberal with his order. He knew I'd be paying. "Eat and be merry, for tomorrow you may diet," he said, his eyes twinkling. When the food arrived, he raised a piece of toast in the air and said, "A toast—to our young guest . . . Crumbs," he added, as it slipped and fell to the table.

"Hey—that's my bread you're spending," I said.

"Don't both of you ever stop?" Rekha asked, not looking totally unamused.

"You gave us a start with that question," Vicky replied. "The answer is, yes, we do, sometimes—to give the other guy a chance." He turned his undivided attention to his food.

"Looking at him eat, you'd think there's a famine on in this country," I remarked, not very imaginatively. But it seemed suddenly very important not to let Vicky steal all the thunder from me in front of Rekha.

"There is, if you'd only read the papers," Vicky retorted, his mouth full.

"How can I—you devour them before I have a chance to," I said, tamely.

"Really?—that's news to me," Vicky replied, and carried on eating.

In short, it was one of those evenings. Somehow when you sit down and try to recollect it afterwards you only remember the worst jokes. Fragments of conversation are embedded in my mind and yet there now seems nothing remarkable about them. Perhaps that is how it always is with personal memories. I don't know why, but when I think of that evening in the café, all I can recall is Rekha sitting in the corner, eyes wide in bemusement, listening avidly to us talking and putting in the occasional flattering comment. It was wonderful—one of those occasions you continue to call memorable long after you have forgotten the details of it.

"What I like about her best," said Vicky after we'd put her in an auto-rickshaw and sent her off home, "is the way she makes you feel important—you know, the way she hangs on to your every word, laughs at your weakest jokes . . . you really feel like a hell of a big wheel when she's around."

"Yeah," I agreed monosyllabically, but a strange emotion was seething within me. I wanted to speak more about her and yet couldn't—for words, I knew, would not be able to bring out the inexplicable feeling of poignant depression that filled me with every thought of her and made each step heavy. She was gone now, and I didn't know when I'd meet her again; yet, after this casual first encounter, I couldn't for the life of me understand why I missed her so much. It was crazy, I told myself: but I wanted to discuss it with Vicky, to talk it over with him and see how he felt about Rekha and the entire situation. But he was soon roped into an impromptu game of cricket on the front lawn, and by the time he returned, was in a different mood, so my questions remained unasked.

The next day there was a quiz on in college. Vicky and I were strolling along to cheer the college team when Rekha appeared around a corner with a bevy of stunning L.W. beauties. They'd all come along for the quiz too, apparently, and we promptly roped them in—two to Vicky's left, two to my right, Rekha in the middle. Somehow the seating just resolved itself, no questions asked, and before I knew it I was leaning over towards her and asking, "How are you?"

"Fine," she whispered back, and it was surprising how a bond seemed to have sprung up between us over the exchange of such inconsequential irrelevancies. I felt a greater intimacy in the friendly smiles that followed than if we had been tossing ardent protestations of love at each other.

"Look at our quiz team," said Vicky, eyeing our representatives with disgust. "It certainly looks very questionable."

Rekha laughed, smiling at him, and I felt a sudden surge of jealousy coursing through me at Vicky thus having impressed her. But I couldn't think of a suitable comeback, and so kept quiet in wordless impotence.

"If ignorance is bliss," Vicky added caustically, "those guys must be very happy indeed."

Rekha laughed again, and this time she was looking into Vicky's eyes. She seemed to find him a wonderful humorist, as did the other girls, who were smilingly awaiting his next *bon mot*.

"Don't tell me this is our 'A' team," said Vicky as our fellows missed out on an answer. "Or is this 'A' team at all?"

Rekha and the girls broke out into peals of laughter so I retorted. "No, that's our 'B' team. Now will you 'B' quiet?"

" 'V' will see about that," he replied promptly. "If 'u' don't mind?"

" 'G', no," I responded rather heavily, "as long as *you* mind your ps and qs."

"OK," said Vicky with an air of finality, and we turned our attention to the quiz again. Nothing would convince the girls that the whole thing had not been planned well in advance!

And I wish it had. Then I might not have let Vicky have the last word.

I really don't know why I'm recounting all this. It is all rather trivial, but then most profound memories are made up of trivia. Anyway you get the picture—a growing triangular closeness, unsurprising because it seemed so natural; a friendship devolving primarily out of silly jokes and chance meetings, as the three of us instinctively reached out for each other's company. And when the quiz, or the debate, or the play, or whatever it was each time, was over, and the meal in the café followed, and Rekha had her customary Coke, and we saw her together to the bus stop or to an auto-rickshaw, even the question "when will we see you again?"

was never asked; somehow it was taken for granted that we would meet, that we would joke, that we would spend a few pleasant minutes or hours in each other's company and go our separate ways, soon to meet again. . . .

But of course that wasn't the full story. There were other things, little things. The smile of admiration that Vicky's jokes elicited from Rekha. The special look in her eye when he bounded up to join us, sweatshirt soaking, from a game of tennis. The way in which she seemed to relish his every casual utterance, while mine were regarded as simply normal. Little things, as I've said, and I did not really resent them: they were barely ripples on the even surface of our tripartite relationship. For I knew they were no threat to me, that Vicky hadn't spent a moment with Rekha in my absence, that all there was to the relationship was what I had participated in. And what could I reproach Vicky for? Rekha meant nothing more to him than an attentive audience for his jokes; she was more intelligent, lively, charming than most, but her attraction, in Vicky's eyes, was not sexual. One day he whisked her hand into his and did a hilarious impression of a lecherous palmist. I could see the flush of embarrassed pleasure mounting on Rekha's cheek, but Vicky was totally unmoved. In his impresario mood, he was the magician, and her hand was his white rabbit, no more, no less. Whereas I would have given anything to have been able to hold the same delicate, long fingers in mine.

Inevitably, things began to change with time. Vicky's interest palled. It was barely noticeable at first, but I was well attuned to the signals—a little tetchiness, a tendency to remember other appointments, a disinclination to shave for the occasion. The ultimate manifestation was when his jokes started declining both in number and in quality. The sure sign that you've lost Vicky is when he no longer wants to try as hard to be funny.

It all came to a head one evening in the café. We were talking, the three of us, desultorily, Rekha sipping tentatively at a Coke while I tried to look into her eyes, and Vicky's attention wandering around the room. Then the far door swung open and the queen of that year's freshman batch walked in. She was bright and statuesque, all flashing eyebrows and pectoral bounce, and she was alone. As she began to look a little uncertainly into the crowd for a friend, Vicky leaped up from his chair and made an unashamed beeline for her. Within minutes he had her enveloped in giggly laughter and had swept her to a corner table for two.

"Looks like Vicky's found another diversion," I said lightly, trying to ignore the look in Rekha's eyes. "Lucky for you I have a one-track mind." She smiled at the weak joke, and suddenly, without any premeditation, I reached forward for her hand where it lay on the tabletop and smothered it in mine. I couldn't think of anything to say.

We looked at each other for what appeared then to me a long moment, but which couldn't have been more than a few seconds. Then, with a sad, almost imperceptible shake of the head, she slowly disengaged her hand from mine.

I don't remember the rest of the conversation. It was awkward, and I recall the sense of relief with which I greeted Vicky, now deprived of his companion, on his return to our table. Yet, when it was time for goodbye, I was left with a bittersweet ache in my mind. I could only think of her, want to be with her, even though she was directly antithetical to all that I had previously looked for in a girl. That evening I was determined to share my feelings with Vicky.

"I rather like Rekha," I said exploratorily, as we strolled to our room after seeing her off in a cab.

"Yes, but if only she wasn't so damned physically unattractive," Vicky replied.

I didn't know what to say. "Yeah, I suppose you're right," I admitted, "but . . ."

"I mean," Vicky added, "I don't think I've ever seen anyone less sexy than dear Rekha. Hell, man—she's got shoulders like a clothes hanger, and there's less on her bosom than in my pockets on a Monday morning."

"Shut up," I said, suddenly venomous. He didn't seem to sense the change in my tone.

"If I took her to our room and the Warden came in, he'd really find a skeleton in our cupboard," added Vicky.

Suddenly, I hit him.

I've never hit anyone before like that, the way I hit him. I'm pretty big, just over six feet, with a cricketer's arms to match, and when I really swing around and hit someone, he stays hit. Vicky reeled back in surprise, his hand to his face, and when he removed his palm there was blood on it.

"Now what did you go and do that for," he said, anguished. For a fleeting second I felt sorry for him; then that emotion was gone, replaced by the same feeling of uncontrollable rage that had made me lash out at him.

"PM, I know I'm a *pun*-y little fellow, but . . ."

"Shut up, Vicky. Shut up, you misbegotten s.o.b., or I swear I'll kill you."

I think I really meant it then—at least I must have sounded like it.

"You bastard. . . ," Vicky whined, but he was scared, and in that apocalyptic moment of realization, I knew he was a coward.

"Shut up, *pun*k," I said, advancing threateningly towards him.

A few guys collected. "Come on, PM, forget it. . . ." they were pushing me away from him.

"You bastard, why don't you pick on someone your own size . . ." He was crying now, and in immeasurable contempt, I turned on my heel and strode off.

Thinking about the whole sordid episode now, I really feel sorry about my impetuosity. I shouldn't have hit him; it wasn't worth it, wasn't worth all the publicity on campus, the pain of separation. I didn't see Rekha again for three months, when we met again at another debate. We said "hello" to each other warmly, exchanged pleasantries, but that was all; there never was anything more to it than that, anyway. I had lost Vicky, and gained nothing. Or maybe I had gained something, a different perspective: that a friend was someone more than just a guy to enjoy jokes with, to go to movies with, to chase girls with—that it was justifiable to demand understanding, empathy . . . or was it? I don't know. Maybe a casual closeness is more important in a college friend than an understanding and a sensitivity that don't in the end change anything. . . .

That evening, I walked to my room, *our* room, opened the lock that Vicky had a spare key to, and let myself in as I had done so often over the past two years. Yet this time it was different. I lay on the bed for a long time, brooding. Darkness fell; I did not switch on the light. A gathering gloom encircled and closed in on me.

Footsteps sounded outside the door. Vicky knocked, formally. "Come in," I said. Vicky came in, walked straight to his suitcase propped up in one corner, and spoke stiffly without looking at me. "I'm moving to the next block. There's a guy there who's willing to share, so I'm pushing in with him." He took off the shirt he was wearing and threw it across to the bed. "Yours," he said briefly. "You've got my shorts on," he added. I remembered I'd run out of undies—they'd accumulated in a corner and I was too lazy to wash them—so I'd borrowed his shorts that morning to use as underwear. I got up, solemnly turned my back to him and took off my trousers. I tossed the shorts to him. They landed in his open suitcase. He shoved them in and shut his suitcase. He looked around to see if there was anything else he'd left behind. His alarm clock—*our* alarm clock—was lying on the bedside table. He picked it up and shoved it inside his bag. The nudie calendar was his; he took it off the wall.

Finally his bag was shut and zipped. He turned to leave: for a second I thought he might say something, some word, some expression, something to remember our two years together by. For a second—but then I realized he was too scared of what I might say or do to speak. I wanted to say something too, but the words stuck in my throat. Wordlessly, he turned, walked through the door, suitcase first, and was gone.

I sat down heavily on the bed, and for the first time in many years, I wept.

1974

The Pyre

He died in my arms that night, died slowly with his head on my lap under the tree into which our scooter had crashed. He moaned once or twice, but his moans were soft, crushed, insensible. I cried then; cried for a friend I knew and loved, who was now slipping away from my life, and from his. His eyes were open as he died, but I don't think he recognized me.

In the morning, when they came with daybreak to the scene of the accident, they found a dead man and a spent one, both silent and unseeing. They had to carry both away, and from a distance it must have been impossible to tell which was the corpse and which the lucky survivor. We shared the single ambulance, he and I, and when I saw him lying there, so near and yet so far away, the memories came flooding back and I wished I could weep. But sorrow required a strength I didn't possess any more. I looked away dry-eyed as the ambulance jolted across Delhi on its futile errand.

All I had was a fracture. The plaster didn't prevent me from either speaking or signing, so the police asked me to do both. He's tired, said the doctor, he's in shock. No, it's all right, I said. Sign here, the inspector said. I signed.

I, Raminder Singh, son of Joginder Singh, residing at E-17, St. Francis' College Hostel, Delhi University, hereby state that on November 3rd inst. at 3:30 a.m., I was riding on a motor scooter driven by Shri Sujeet Kumar, student, who did not possess a license for the same. While on the Ridge, Shri Kumar, who was in a state of partial intoxication, lost control of the scooter, left the roadway, and struck a tree. He was not wearing a crash helmet. . . .

I didn't recall putting it quite that way. "Lost control of the scooter?" Or had I said that Sujeet, to avoid what he thought was a black cat crossing his path, had swerved to one side and crashed head first into a branch? The cat didn't exist, not outside of Sujeet's imagination, but the branch did, and it shouldn't have been there, practically overhanging the road. Somebody who was supposed to trim it had screwed up, inspector. Had screwed us up. I fell off the pillion onto my arse but Sujeet flew over the handlebars onto his head. Sure he was a little stoned, but it was that branch that did us in. No, he didn't have a license, but there was nothing wrong with his driving, inspector. No, the scooter didn't belong to him. No, its owner was unaware that we were using it. But what are you saying, inspector? Sujeet's dead! He's dead, inspector, and you're asking about Bobby's scooter?

"Poor Bobby's going to blow up" had been my first thought when we hit the tree. It wasn't the first time we had borrowed Bobby's scooter, and he'd never noticed. We knew he was so possessive about the damned thing, and it was just a question of whacking the keys from his desk while he was sleeping and wheeling the scooter out of the shed past the *chowkidar*, who'd been given a packet of Charminar to look the other way. As I said, we'd done it before; it was nothing new. But with each successive trip we'd been less careful.

But Sujeet drove bloody well for a guy who did all his driving on the sly. And on a high.

"State of partial intoxication." That was a laugh. He'd had

enough grass for three cows. Which is why he started seeing black cats on the road when you could barely see the road itself. "Hey," he'd called out in that half-crazy way of his, "hey—I don't want that black cat crossing our path, that's bad luck. I'm going to go right round him and beat that son-of-a-bitch to it—watch." My yell of protest was drowned by the extra revving of the motor. And cut short as we crashed into that tree.

I began swearing as soon as I got my breath back and could feel the soreness of my arse and the pain in my leg. "I can't stand up, you stupid bugger," I screamed. "You've broken my frigging leg, you bastard!"

But the expected reply in kind didn't come. After a minute or two I stopped swearing and looked in his direction. He was lying horribly still. I started calling out to him then, softly at first, then more insistently, but there was no response. I crawled towards him, dragging myself along on my good leg. He didn't answer me. My elbows were hurting and there was a gash on my right arm, and the pain in my behind sent shock waves through me with each forward thrust of my body, but finally I reached him. He was still breathing—I remember that, and the brief sense of relief I felt. I put out a hand to touch him and felt the terrible warm stickiness of his blood. It was then that he moaned, for the first time. And I knew my nightmare had begun.

I moved my hands and felt blood everywhere I touched. I called out to him, shouting loudly, and tried to shake him back to life. Nothing, not even a moan this time. I tried to recollect anything I'd ever read or heard about first aid. My mind remained blank. God, I wished I wasn't draxed, I couldn't even think properly and I. . . . I had to help him. That was all I could think of. I had to help him. I collapsed onto my arse and dragged his head onto my lap. He moaned again. I shouted once, twice, into the stillness of the night. It was of no use. No one was going to be on the Ridge at that time. I thought vaguely of going and calling for help, but the pain told me I couldn't get very far. And where, when, how could

I go? The best way I could help was to hold his head on my lap and give him comfort until help arrived at daybreak.

And Sujeet lay dying on my lap.

The postmortem called it a brain hemorrhage. The concussion had been so severe, the fat, balding and antiseptic doctor told me at the hospital with his paw on my shoulder, that he would never have been normal again even if he had recovered. So perhaps, the doctor blinked behind owlish glasses, perhaps it was better this way. I nodded and wormed away from his patronizing hand.

His parents came by the first train. Poor people. They had struggled so much to give Sujeet an education at the best places, to fight for every seat, every quota that their untouchability entitled them to. He had always made the grade, and they must have been so proud of his English, his jeans, his upper-caste friends, his Zapata moustache, quite unlike any Harijan boy they had ever known. And now. . . . He was their only son, their only hope in an unjust world, the eldest in a family of daughters, the blessed future provider. He was dead.

He had always made the grade, but he had never conformed: he had realized early that his devilry was what made him acceptable to his peers. There were other Scheduled Caste boys at college, small, dark, mousy scholars who spoke when they were spoken to and sat by themselves at mealtimes. Sujeet was not like them. He cut classes, interjected at campus debates, chased girls. And took drugs.

I guess it was I who first got him into it, though it could have been any of us. I remember, though, his hesitation at the outstretched joint in my hand. I'll never know now whether it was at the act of drug-taking or at the prospect of putting his mouth to something being smoked by a Jat and about to be passed on to a Brahmin. He hesitated, and then through the swirling mists in my mind I remember someone's curled lip and the words, "what's the matter—scared?" He took the joint from me immediately, and it was as if he was laying everything he'd ever feared on the line.

I wanted to say something to his parents. Sujeet wasn't afraid; he wasn't afraid of the things you are afraid of. But I didn't, because I couldn't; and because I knew that if he had stayed afraid, had not dared, had not chosen to defy every convention the world had thrust upon him, he might have been alive.

And then I thought of Mira. Mira, the girl he screwed and I wished I could; Mira, the General's daughter, sultry, exciting, unattainable Mira. Mira, of the dark eyes and the painted, carefully-shaped eyebrows, of the hip-hugging pants and sleeveless shirts that somehow never reached her waist and gave me so many tantalizing views of the small of her back; what would this do to Mira? Mira who was so much in love with the one guy who didn't give a damn about her, Mira who defied society with a toss of her head and bedded the grandson of a cobbler, Mira who let him hump her regularly in the little room next to mine in the dormitory while I sat on my side of the wall and tried to read—what would Mira do?

I'd have to be the one to tell her. To say that Sujeet wasn't going to be at the back gate of her dorm the next day. To inform her about the funeral.

The funeral. The funeral will be held this evening at 4:00 p.m. at Haldi Ghat, the college announced. I didn't want to go. How could I go there and see a friend I'd been talking, laughing, joking, smoking with for the last three years being burned to ashes? At four o'clock we should have been in the café together, not at some crematorium with one of us dead. It just didn't make any sense.

The only funeral I'd ever attended was my grandfather's. They'd called me from school after my last exam and told me in hushed tones that it had happened at last, and I had to rush home. The Sikh driver from the office was there, and instead of his usual indifference, he picked me up very tenderly and put me by his side on the front seat of the car. When I got home there was a crowd of people, mostly subordinates who'd envied him and competitors who'd hated his guts, standing around in the living room looking suitably grieved. And there was mother in the bedroom trying to console grandma, who was weeping bitter tears into the end of her sari, wailing so loudly it was embarrassing, while my father, his face set, sat completely still by grandfather's bed, as if still maintaining the vigil the family had kept for the last eight weeks. And I, the only one who'd really ever loved grandfather, the only one he'd always got along with and whose company he could bear, I wasn't allowed in to pay my last respects because the sight of death was considered too much for my eleven-year-old sensibilities.

But I saw him at the funeral, lying on his bier, triumphant in death as in life. He had had plenty of time to meet his end, to make his will and issue his last instructions before handing over the firm to my father. He was over seventy and had lived a full life, and his final illness, when it came, had not ravaged him. Even in death his face bore the look of arrogant self-confidence it had always done; no crease of pain marred those perfect, haughty, aristocratic features. It was a fitting way to go, and I had the sense of participating in a moving, but not sad, family ritual as I stood behind my father and he held my fingers tightly in one hand while he lit the pyre with the other.

That was what death and funerals should be about. Not this.

"Ram, you son-of-a-bitch," Sujeet had said once. "I know what a lot of you guys thought about me when I first got into this elite little college of yours. One more *chamar* on an affirmative action program, right? Wouldn't even have got in if the government hadn't obliged the college to reserve a couple of seats for the Scheduled Castes. Well, I don't give a shit what those turds think, or you too, for that matter. It's my right, my right and that of my people, because you bastards have got to pay for centuries of bloody discrimination. And I'm going to enjoy that right, Ram, and I'm not going to be apologetic about it. I'm going to enjoy everything this bloody college has to offer, the library, the theater, the rich buggers' motorbikes, the booze and the parties—and I'm going to enjoy the girls. And then I'm going to go right on to the bloody Indian bloody Administrative Service, and I'm going to get a posting to my family's home district. No Foreign Service for me, my friend, no fobbing off the untouchable with offers of New York or Paris, no sir. I'm going to be District Magistrate in Chhoti Haveli and I'm going to get every bloody Jat and Thakur in the area to kiss my arse. You just watch me, Ram my friend. You just watch me." And he had taken another drag, and he had turned smiling to me and said, "And you know what? At the end of the whole bloody thing, when I'm finally dead and gone, bloody Brahmins are going to come to my funeral."

They came. Most of the college dorm was there at Haldi Ghat. So was I. I stood there with Mira sobbing softly into my shoulder and stared glassy-eyed at the funeral pyre while I patted her silky head in sympathy. His parents wept openly, and the little knot of Harijan scholars stood in a solemn circle away from the rest. The priests talked among themselves, and chanted, and pulled out the tins of *vanaspati*. As they poured it into the crackling fire the flames leaped higher, enveloping the body in its shroud under the wood. And the smoke that was Sujeet rose towards the sky.

1973

The Political Murder

As a policeman I make it a point to steer clear of politicians. Being a servant of the state has its advantages, but then silver linings do have their clouds and a cop's special cloud is his local politician. One of my erstwhile colleagues posted in a rural *tehsil* once complained ruefully over a pint of beer in the Policemen's Club that whenever the resident MLA's foot wasn't in his mouth it was usually treading on the inspector's corns. Being based in the city has its compensations but hasn't endeared me any more to the denizens of our democracy. In the force one of the first things you learn is to mind your own business. As far as politicians went I was only too happy to observe the rule.

Till Gobinda Sen got himself murdered.

Gobinda Sen was a member of the West Bengal Legislative Assembly and had a house in Calcutta though he was elected from some mofussil district or the other. As with many MLAs of his type he shuttled back and forth between his city home and his rural constituency. This year he was back in the capital for the budget session. I don't much care for the political news, but I couldn't help noticing how frequently his name appeared in the newspaper reports of the legislators' discussions on the budget proposals. Gobinda Babu, as he was known, was an influential and strong-willed politician, a man widely respected on both the Treasury and the Opposition benches. And, on the morning something jammed the silencer of my scooter and I reported five minutes late for work at the HQ, he was dead.

The boss wasn't amused. In moments of deep emotion his vocabulary ranges from late Victorian to early Zane Grey.

"Nayar, you misbegotten son-of-a-bee," he said cordially when I apologetically answered his summons, "you're supposed to be on duty, not taking a promenade down the Strand to meet a dilatory sweetheart. Gobinda Sen's been murdered this morning and the DIG's having kittens. A jeep's leaving in about thirty seconds for his Alipur bungalow, and you're supposed to be on it. Now haul your *a* out of this *o* before I kick you in the *p*."

One thing they teach you in the force is politeness, manners, refinement. I saluted, smiled an off-duty grin, and left.

Gobinda Sen's one-storied bungalow was a little way off the road and was approached by a longish drive which wound its way through an unusually well-maintained garden. The place was surrounded by a ten-foot wall opening out in two gates, each with a *durwan*, the IN gate possessing in addition a sentry box, where visitors stated name, occupation, and purpose of visit. In our case, of course, there was no need for the formalities. The news wasn't supposed to have broken but the place was already teeming with people and cars that looked as if they belonged to people who were important or thought they should be. The gates were shut to keep them out, but the *durwans* were plainly having a tough time. A preliminary police team had already arrived when the murder was first discovered earlier in the morning, and three of them had stayed back pending our arrival.

As soon as we drove in through the gate, ignoring the shouted questions of the crowd outside, the short, harried-looking sub-inspector in charge waddled up to me. "Inspector Nayar," he said, his hand in salutation touching a perspiring brow, "I'm Sub-Inspector Jacob. The body's upstairs. Nothing's been touched, everything's been left for your team. Shall we climb the stairs?" He glanced briefly at me for confirmation, knowing that none was necessary, and turned to the staircase. Havildar Ghosh, my right-hand man, parked the jeep and joined us. Followed by our squad of experts, we climbed up to the MLA's bedroom.

"I'll fill you in on some of the details briefly," Jacob said as we ascended the steps. "Gobinda Sen came back late last night from an after-dinner meeting—a political one, something about what's on in the Vidhan Sabha nowadays. The *durwan* opened the gate for him after midnight. He let himself into his house—the household was asleep. Not that there's very many of them—Gobinda Babu was a bachelor, lived alone, just a cook and a houseboy and a handyman, whose wife also functions as a sort of maid. They all sleep downstairs; there are no servants' quarters as such but then there's enough space in the house for a bachelor—most of the rooms are guest rooms. Anyway, the houseboy usually wakes him up every morning with his bed-tea. Today he knocked as usual at 7:30. He has standing instructions to wake up Gobinda Babu at 7:30 whatever hour of the previous night he goes to sleep. There was no reply, but this wasn't surprising; most people who are regularly woken up develop a tendency to oversleep till they are. So he turned the handle—and found this."

We'd reached the bedroom already, and Jacob casually, almost routinely, pushed open the door. I've seen plenty of cadavers in my time, but I haven't ceased being sickened by what one human being can do to another. Gobinda Sen lay on his bed, *dhoti* in disarray, soaked in blood. There was a knife sticking out of him, but at first glance it was obvious that the wound it was embedded in was not the only one that had caused his death. Holes gaped in his *kurta* and the exposed portions of his body, holes covered and ringed by russet-red circlets of congealed blood. He had been dead some time.

The doctor from our squad didn't take long to examine the body. "He's been dead almost ten hours," he said.

"I didn't need you to tell me that," I retorted. "He hadn't changed out of his *dhoti-kurta*—must have been killed soon after his return. Fingerprints?"

The fingerprint man, who had looked carefully at the knife, shook his head. I wasn't surprised. People who use knives aren't stupid enough to do so without taking some kind of precaution.

"Eyes open," added the doctor. "Wasn't killed suddenly or while sleeping. Evidence of struggle—or at least he seems to have thrashed about a bit."

"Thanks again," I rejoined ungratefully. "The bedclothes are messed up enough anyway—even I could deduce someone had either an orgy or a struggle on the bed. Leave the poor chap alone," I added. "Ghosh, cover him up."

I stepped past the bed to the window. The pane was shattered, glass lay in fragments all over the balcony, and little slivers were embedded on the bedroom carpet beneath it. The point of entry. Perhaps.

"Check for footprints," I barked. But I didn't expect too much. There would be none on the carpet; a careful assassin needn't have left any on the balcony either. I wasn't too surprised when the eventual answer came like a development in a darkroom: negative.

I looked out the window. A drainpipe, almost perfectly positioned for a murderer, ran down the wall to the garden. Apart from a few bushes and a solitary neem tree, nothing stood between the house and the road but the surrounding ten-foot wall, which could easily be scaled via the tree. The bedroom window overlooked the other portion of the house: it was not visible from either gate, and at night the streetlights were unlikely to reach and illuminate it. I turned back in disgust.

"What a setup," I growled at no one in particular. "Out here he was about as safe as the swimmers in *Jaws*."

I looked around the room; Ghosh and two of the others had

already beaten me to it. "I checked as well," interposed Sub-Inspector Jacob, "without disturbing anything, of course. There's nothing of any interest." He waved me to a chair and sank on one himself, looking very tired and very unhappy. "What a case," he lamented loudly. "I don't envy you a moment of it. Anyone could have killed him—the opportunity was scarcely lacking. And the motive—a man like this, a politician of standing and influence, helpful to many people, dangerous to others: it must have been so easy to make enemies. But you've got to do something impressive because the man—was—an MLA."

He mopped his brow. "So you have to find, in a metropolis of eight million, the man or men who jumped over a wall, broke a window, killed a politician, and shoved off—leaving no clues except for an eight-anna knife bought from a roadside vendor on Dharamtolla." He sighed expressively. "What a case," he repeated.

"I don't know," I said, slowly, playing with the embroidery on the armrest of my chair. Talking to people about a case once I'm on it often helps me to marshal my thoughts, clear my mind of the tangled webs of unsorted facts that impinge when one is faced with so much so suddenly under such pressure. Havildar Ghosh, who'd worked with me as long as I'd been on the force, understood this and stood respectfully by listening "To my mind there are a few disturbing aspects to this case. Which doesn't mean I agree or disagree entirely with what you've said; you're right, this is going to be a tough nut to crack precisely because it's so open. But I'm not happy about a few things. I can understand the *durwan* at the gate not hearing the breaking of the windowpane—there's the distance, and then *durwans* do sleep, for God's sake, it isn't a crime. But how is it that with all these people sleeping downstairs no one heard the murdered man's cries? He must have cried—he couldn't not have; if he'd died with the first stroke, the subsequent ones wouldn't have been needed. Yes, yes, I know the objections you'll raise: the air-conditioning was on, the door was shut, the people were in all probability asleep. But I can accept one person not hearing, two even, but four? Surely at least one of them might have been a light sleeper? Oh, of course these are just suspicions, born out of my basically very suspicious nature—I don't know, perhaps I'm just wasting my time. But let me talk to these people."

The houseboy, obviously very upset, eyes still red with crying, was the first to come in. "Houseboy" was an anomalous term for him; he must have been at least sixty, an old and trusted retainer who'd worked with Gobinda Babu for over a decade, ever since he had become an MLA. He confirmed Jacob's earlier version of his story, only it was more pathetic to see him, broken and old, weeping every time he thought of his master, punctuating his narrative with wails of how good a man Gobinda Babu was and how could anybody have murdered him. It was all very sad, and I felt a strong surge of sympathy flow through me, but only for a moment. One can't afford to be a sympathetic policeman, not if one has a murder on one's hands. In a terrible pun I've ever since been ashamed of, I'd once observed that a policeman had to be a copper, but the aesthetics of humor apart, I was grateful for that reserve of copperlike hardness as I turned to question the old man.

"What were you doing when the master came in last night?"

"I . . . I . . . was . . . asleep." The words came out in a racking sob, as if the man wished he had been awake so that he could have been of some use. "I sleep in the little room downstairs in the corner."

"You heard nothing?"

"I am an old man. I heard nothing."

I dismissed him with a caution that I might need him later.

There was little I could ask the cook. He too had been asleep, he too had heard nothing. But he didn't break down and weep, like the houseboy; he was calmer, quieter. He had been, as I would say in my report, in the employ of the deceased for the past five years.

"Tell me—what do you think of your master? Would anyone want to murder him?"

"He was a good man," the cook said simply. "I do not know about his political foes, but I do know that he never hurt another person if he could help it. He was sincere, honest, well-liked. In this world such people are not necessarily safe."

"No," I said, looking him full in the face. "Such people are not necessarily safe." I stared at him for a full moment and he returned my look quietly, unflinchingly. "You may go now," I said. "But don't leave the house. You will have to come to the police station to record your statement."

The handyman came in with his wife, the maid. The woman was obviously shaken; she seemed terrified out of her wits and her eyes, too, were red and swollen. I let her sit while her tall, broad, oddly bespectacled husband stood, and went over the by-now-familiar ground. They too had been asleep, they too had heard nothing. But they at least had the excuse that they had been together.

"You're terribly upset," I remarked kindly to the woman.

She seemed startled, "No—of course not. I mean yes, of course, how can I not be upset when a murder has been committed in this very house." She looked over her shoulder to where Gobinda Babu still lay, covered now with a spotless white sheet, and there was a look in her eyes that bordered on fear.

"Of course," I said slowly. Then, after a pause—"Were you very close to him?"

"What do you mean?" Her voice was shaking. "I was his maid."

I looked up at her husband for a long while, then turned back to her. "Yes, of course," I said. "You were his maid." I didn't wait for that to sink in. "What did you think of Gobinda Babu?" I asked the husband. "Why would anyone want to murder him?"

"He had many enemies," came the reply. The handyman looked me squarely in the face, eyes blinking occasionally behind the spectacles. "Many enemies. But he was a good man," he added. "A good man. Very decent to us he has been. But he was a big man—a very big man. And big men have enemies."

"Tell me," I said to the woman, anxious to corroborate part of the houseboy's narrative, "how did you both come to know of the murder?"

"The way the cook also did," answered her husband. "Gopal, the houseboy, saw the body and screamed. At least he says he did—none of us heard him, but then we were downstairs in our rooms. Then he came rushing down wailing. He woke up the cook first, screaming. "The master's been murdered. Murdered." That's all he said, he wasn't coherent at all. My wife was shocked into hysterics, and I stayed with her while the cook called the police. Then you," he indicated Sub-Inspector Jacob, "arrived and it was the cook who showed you the room. This is the first time both of us have even come up here today. My wife was inconsolable—she can't stand the sight of blood. She even fainted once when I cut my hand," he added conversationally. "She wouldn't have dreamed of coming here with all that blood. I remember once. . . ."

"H'm," I interrupted unkindly. "We haven't the time for your little domestic details. I'm more interested in your account of the houseboy's reaction to his discovery. He said 'The master's murdered, murdered' didn't he? You said he was incoherent—how incoherent was he?"

"That's all he said," replied the handyman. "He kept saying 'the master's murdered, murdered' over and over again and sobbing. It took him quite a while to calm down. At first we couldn't understand what had happened, but the word 'murdered' was enough—enough for my wife to go to pieces, poor girl, and for the cook to ring up the cops—sorry, I mean you gentlemen."

" 'The master's murdered, murdered,' " I mused. "That's all? Over and over again? He didn't give you any further details? Gruesome descriptions?"

"Oh, no, certainly not," the handyman replied. "He wasn't in a condition to do so."

"Yes, of course," I said, suddenly, incredibly, human. "I understand."

When they left Sub-Inspector Jacob gave me a quizzical look. "And how does all that help?" he asked, with only the barest deference due my rank. "Seems to me we're back where we started."

"Does it really, Sub-Inspector?" I settled myself more comfortably in my chair. "Will you tell me why you say that?"

"Well, their stories have given you nothing to go on—no fresh clue, and no earthly reason why any of these people should have wanted to murder a man they'd worked with for long and appear to be fond of. Or do they?"

"Really, Sub-Inspector? You don't think we've gained anything these last forty-five minutes? I'd beg to disagree. Let's review the situation. A man's murdered, someone's stuck a knife in him about thirteen times, and because he's a politician we immediately come to the conclusion it's a political murder. Need it be? When someone dies of thirteen wounds, he's either been killed by thirteen people, like some kind of latter-day Julius Caesar, or by someone who's so bloody furious with him he can't stop striking. And politically, Gobinda Sen was not the man to attract that kind of viciousness, at least not from what I know of his politics. But personally? That's another matter. A bachelor, living alone, a scrupulously organized reticence surrounding his personal life—who's to know whether some man hates his guts or not? I prefer to work on the suspicion that someone did—that this was what the French so often call a crime of passion, not a careful, premeditated murder. In which case it would have had to be perpetrated by someone inside the house." I paused, looked around. Jacob was interested, not yet convinced, Ghosh was nodding his approbation—he knew the direction my thoughts were taking.

"The cook, the houseboy—obviously innocent. But the handyman: not so easily exonerated. Nothing I could place my finger on: certainly no motive. Till the woman provided me with one. The moment I asked her about Sen she committed the fatal error of overreacting to my not-too-subtle insinuation. It all fitted in: an illicit relationship, dramatic discovery by the husband, impassioned murder, and hasty cover-up: just the kind of thing cases are made of in the detective novels. But absolutely no proof, of course.

"Then I started scenting a trail when the husband deliberately tried to attribute the murder to political opposition—'big men have enemies.' In his anxiety to lead me onto the wrong track, he unfortunately talked too much. He spoke of his wife being unable to stand the sight of blood—yet from what the houseboy had told him how did he know there was any blood at all? Gobinda Sen had been 'murdered'; he could have been strangled, asphyxiated, gassed, anything. Yet our friend the handyman knew there was blood. Which meant he'd done the killing."

There was a stunned silence in the room.

"I can just imagine it," I added, ever unable to resist the melodramatic. "Gobinda Sen comes home at night, expecting perhaps to find the maid waiting for him. Perhaps she is—but so is her husband. He is pushed onto the bed and stabbed with a cuckold's fury. The terrified wife acquiesces in the *fait accompli* and helps cover it up. But neither performs the task too well."

"And the window?" asked Sub-Inspector Jacob. "What about the window?"

"Ah, the window," I smiled. "Ask the handyman to come in again."

This time he was scared. You could see the fear in the rapid blinking of his eyes behind the heavy frame of his glasses. I stepped up to him, smiled pleasantly, and removed the spectacles from his nose. Then, quite deliberately, I flicked my index finger hard at the lens. The glass shattered and fell at his feet. A couple of fragments lay on my foot.

"Hey—what did you do that f. . . ." he began.

"To show you where you went wrong in breaking the windowpane," I said harshly. "When I broke your lens from this side most of the glass fell near you. When our mysterious murderer broke the windowpane, ostensibly to get in, the broken glass equally mysteriously opted for the balcony instead of the bedroom carpet. Which means the murderer didn't break it to get in. He was trying to be smart, trying to set up an interesting but misleading clue to disguise a murder that had been committed by someone who had no need to break any windows. You."

"Oh my God," he said as the handcuffs went on.

"You'll have plenty of time to be devout in the Central Jail," I remarked cheerfully. "Right now you'd better pray for a speedy trial. Come on, Ghosh."

It was a few years later, when Jacob had become a deputy commissioner of police and I was still an inspector, that I let my resentments overcome my natural reticence late one evening at the Policemen's Club. We'd been drinking together, me a few glasses too many, and what sparked it was something as innocent as Jacob reaching forward to sign my chit.

"Hey, let me . . . ," I began, then checked myself. "What the hell," I said. "On what you earn nowadays, why the hell shouldn't you pick up the tab?"

Jacob looked embarrassed, but I went on, my speech slurring. "Look at the way they reward talent in this bloody force," I said bitterly. "Take a man like me, knows his work, doesn't lick any asses—so no promotion in eleven years. And you, Jacob—respectful, well-behaved, but you couldn't spot a clue if it hit you in the face—and it's I who've got to salute you."

"Now that's not quite fair," he began, a little heatedly. I cut him short.

"Take the Gobinda Sen case, for instance," I said. "Most celebrated murder in Calcutta for years, and I solve it in a morning, while you went around bleating you had no leads. What happens? Do I get so much as a thank you? No sir—it's you who get the promotion. Bloody hell." I signaled sloppily for another drink.

Jacob banged his glass down, his face darkening. "All right, you poor sap," he glowered. "You asked for it. So you think you're the hero of the Gobinda Sen case, do you? Well, let me tell you something. The myopic hulk you've had put away in Central Jail didn't do it."

"What?" I looked at him in disbelief. "You must be mad. You testified in court that . . ."

"Sure I did. But that's got nothing to do with anything."

"But—his wife—I could have sworn . . ."

"Okay, so maybe she was warming Gobinda Sen's bed for him. So what? Her husband was doing pretty well out of the arrangement, in any case. He wasn't going to erupt in a burst of jealous rage after tolerating it for years."

"But . . . the blood . . . how did he know about the blood?"

"He didn't know about the blood, Nayar. All he said was that he and his wife hadn't gone up to the room because she was inconsolable. Then he probably realized what that implied, so he covered up by adding that crap about the blood—on the basis of the mess he was seeing around him while talking to you. But you're so smart, of course, that you read even more into his statement than he intended to conceal."

"But who—what—I don't understand." I stuttered lamely.

"That's exactly your problem, Nayar," Jacob said softly. "You don't understand. You think you do, but you don't really. And that's why we needed you that day. We needed someone with your capacity for self-deception."

"We—who's we?"

"Guess, Nayar, just guess," Jacob replied. "Maybe you should start paying a little more attention to politics instead of playing Sherlock Holmes all the time. Then maybe you'll become deputy commissioner one day."

1975

The Other Man

I know your name almost as well as my own. Arvind. Sometimes she cries it out at night when she is with me on my bed. Arvind. How I have grown to hate that name.

I know what you look like. I see you in my nightmares, in the other half of my mind when I think of her. I see you in her eyes when she speaks of you, and you are a wall between us I cannot surmount. If we pass each other on the street one day I know I will spot you. You will look like a man who feels he ought to be recognized.

I know how wonderful you are. What a heart of gold God has blessed you with. How you smile, how your teeth flash in the sun and your eyes twinkle as you toss your hair back from your forehead and walk towards her. She tells me of you sometimes, and when she speaks she looks indescribably beautiful, head partially bowed, eyes far away, lips moving quietly in remembrance, and I yearn to touch that loose curling strand of hair that falls on her cheek, but know I cannot reach her. And despite her beauty she is frightening then, lost to me, as I sit there next to her and see how distant you can make her. She sits wrapped in a tender, impenetrable cocoon of remembered love. And I am afraid.

I am afraid when I hold her hand and fear yours was not as sweaty. I am afraid when I turn to her in love and call her by a name she has heard more often from your lips. I am afraid when I disrobe before her and wonder whether you were stronger, taller, better-built than I am. I am afraid when she holds my face in her soft hands and looks into my eyes, for I do not know what she sees there, myself or the ghost of your memory. And I cringe when sometimes in the dark, that great leveler, she shudders beneath my touch and cries your name. Alone with her, I fear the night.

And I fear you. I fear you not as a remnant of a past that was beautiful and personal and very, very happy, a past I cannot deny her because it is a part of her life, of what she is to me. But I fear you instead as a looming, threatening shadow that might one day emerge from her past into my present, emerge to shatter the little world I have created for myself and her. For I know and she knows and we both acknowledge that you have a prior claim on her that I can never supersede. You are the first man she gave herself to. And she was yours till you left her.

Till you left her. Left her for the attractions of an alien land where there was money and pride and that intangible thing you termed satisfaction. Left her with a ring and a promise you would return to redeem the pledge it represented. And she let you go, accepting your departure as unavoidable, refusing to be tempted into hoping for your return. Because she loved you.

But she waited. That was the tragedy of it all, she waited. For what, she did not know. But she waited, and while I came to love her and seek her for myself, she would not give herself to me. She was yours, and in her waiting she remained yours.

Then, little by little, she succumbed. Succumbed to a woman's need to be wanted and loved and cared for. But she never let me forget, with each iota of her resistance that gave way, that she was not mine. And as I tried to place the shroud of my affections over her, to cover her with a love that would shut out the pressures of external things, I realized the shattering truth. The truth that while her body, her time, her nominal existence, might be given to me, her mind and heart were still waiting. For you.

I did not know how long she would wait. How long she could wait. But then she herself did not know what she was waiting for. As time passed I began to hope that its passage would slowly eradicate, if not the memory, the need to sustain it. Loving her, I slowly learned not to expect anything in return, or even from myself. All along I was gentle and loving and patient. And all broken up inside.

Then you wrote. Telling her you were alive and doing well and you still cared. Or thought you cared. And presuming with the easy confidence of long possession that she was still yours, that she had not changed. I remember her face the day she got your letter. With your casual, effortless words you touched a chord in her I had never been able to feel. Quietly, that evening, soundlessly giving vent to a pain I knew she felt deeper inside than I had ever seen, she wept. And she cried for you in my arms.

She did not reply to your letter. And yet with that nongesture she seemed only to grow even more remote from me, remote and beautiful and so much more in need of the love I was so willing to give her. I loved her then in a strange, new kind of way, as one loves a finely-turned sentence in a book that one wishes one could write but knows one can't. It was easier then to be reconciled to her inaccessibility. For perhaps that was what made her what she was, a Mona Lisa. And I could never reach her smile.

Every time I touched her it was a commitment, a commitment not to possess. And when your second letter came, and she did not reply to that one too, I knew in a strange way that it only reaffirmed the terms of my commitment. You did not write again. And if you had, perhaps she still would not reply. But she is still waiting.

And that is why I still fear you. For as long as you remain away and tell her you love her from the other end of a postage stamp I know I can still preserve my tenuous hold on the reality of her life. But I am afraid that you may not. I am afraid that one day you will step out of the murky, half-light of remembered importance and enter the harsher glare of tomorrow's sun. And then I do not know what will happen to me.

But perhaps you will not. Perhaps she will go on waiting for that something within her to break or bloom. Perhaps one day it will, and it will not be you effecting the change but I and my relationship with her. Yes, I too will wait and hope. For I know that there is one thing in her you will never understand. That the ring she wears on her second finger is not yours but mine. That the surname she bears today is not the one you wrote on the airmail envelope you addressed to her but the one I signed on our marriage register. That she chose at all to marry me when she was still yours. For there is one thing I know that you will never learn and that the world will never tell you. That six months after she became my wife, she bore me your son.

1974

Auntie Rita

Having an affair with your aunt is fraught with a lot of serious complications. At least that's what Arjun discovered when he went down to Calcutta to spend his autumn holidays with Auntie Rita and realized that he loved her.

As realizations go, it was a pretty significant one in his life, and as realizations don't go, this one stayed in the innermost recesses of his mind and grew. Actually it hadn't quite dawned on him slowly, in the manner of most pansophisms. He had always had a lurking suspicion he was in love with somebody, and the day before his departure for Calcutta his rejection by the fat-arsed, bosomy nymphet who lived downstairs confirmed that she couldn't possibly have been the queen of his heart. Which left only Auntie Rita in his brief roster of attractive members of the opposite sex.

Not that his love for her was the result of any logical or even consciously biological process. In fact it had only been on that second evening on the terrace that he had come to realize it was she his heart thirsted after.

Why? Arjun often asked himself the question, so often that he began to sound like a child who had forgotten the last letter of the alphabet. Why? Why? Each time Arjun found himself stumped for a reply. What was it in her that really attracted him? That astonishing freshness of face in a thirty-two-year-old given to a generosity around the hips and waistline that came from fourteen years of indolent housewifery and no children; that provocative, even slightly promiscuous tilt of her face as she talked, despite the overwhelming respectability of marriage and aunthood; the even greater eloquence of her elegantly *kaajal*ed eyes that gazed into his, frankly admiring his cherubic good looks though she'd first seen him as a runny-nosed three-year-old when she'd married his uncle; which of all these caused fluttering fingers to clutch at his heart and his femur and fibula to turn into gelatine, Arjun did not know. All of them, perhaps—and yet, at the same time, maybe none of them. . . .

"What's a man without an ego?" she'd said unblushingly to him that evening on the terrace, as the lengthening shadows closed in on them and the rooftops of Calcutta retaliated with intermittent yellow spots of electric lighting, and she looked straight into a face that had not yet learned to dissemble its feelings. Perhaps that was where Rita really scored, in her sense of time and place and appropriateness and her vital grasp of what exactly to say that would have the most telling effect. Maybe her psychology lectures at Women's Christian College years ago had been of some use after all; or maybe it was simply an inherent gift, some kind of an acquired art that made her a mistress of the business of capturing seventeen-year-old hearts by appealing to the postpubescent vanity that pulses in them.

"What's a man without an ego?" To Arjun the question seemed profound, yet self-answering, as if there could really be no doubt about its meaning: nothing, of course. He gazed at her with deep respect, not simply because of what she'd said but because of its applicability to him, and not just because it flattered his own vanity but because it legitimized what he had often been told was his own most glaring defect. The sin of self-obsession attributed to him by the well-rounded nymphet could now be washed away in the purificatory waters of the all-excusing ego. What a difference between Auntie Rita and the girl at home; what a difference between a mature, wise woman of the world and a flighty sixteen-year-old slattern who flirted with you and never gave you a chance to find out where exactly you stood with her. . . .

"It's seven. Shall we go down?" Arjun nodded, his reverie shattered, and instinctively glanced at his watch, a prophylactic move for self-protection that froze stillborn as Auntie Rita lost her footing for a moment and fell heavily against him. In the same moment she recovered her step, even before Arjun could start to make a move to hold her protectively and prevent a fall, but the feel of her body still lingered against his. Blood pounding, he followed her swaying hips and dangling plait down the steep stairway that led to her flat.

Auntie Rita. Somehow, despite everything, it had first come as a bit of a shock to him to feel sexually aroused by his uncle's wife. All his seventeen years of disciplined obedience to parental dicta made his overexercised conscience initially rebel against the thought. I mean, all I'd have to do would be to hit her first to add incest to injury, he rather facetiously told himself, arguing futilely against the stirrings of his incipient id. But it didn't work. When you're seventeen, and just discovering your masculinity, few things stand in the way of a potential sexual adventure, even if it's with your aunt—in this case, especially if it's with your aunt.

Even then, coming to Calcutta to spend his autumn holidays—the "Puja vacations," they called it in Bengal—with his uncle hadn't been his idea. His uncle, a diffident, good-natured, insecure introvert with a vague and troublesome sense of familial responsibility, had invited him down more because it was the expected avuncular thing to do rather than out of any particular fondness for his precocious nephew. But since he didn't expect a refusal, and was kind enough not to hint he'd welcome one, he didn't get any. Arjun came to Calcutta, lock, stock, and shaving-set (freshly purchased, locally-made, never used), and announced his intention of staying two weeks. Then, on the second day of Arjun's mildly uneventful stay, Uncle Kumar was suddenly called away on a business trip. After a brief moment of panic—disruptions of schedule rarely featured in the Kumar routine of existence—Auntie Rita and Arjun helped him pack, and drove him in the '64 two-door Herald (which Rita managed pretty well) to the station.

"I'll try to get back as soon as possible," Kumar had said nervously through the bars of his first-class compartment just before his train left. "Look after Arjun, Rita," he'd yelled as an afterthought when the train moved away.

"I will," she shouted back, but he was too far away by then to see the strange light in her eyes.

On their return she'd suggested a short walk on the terrace. "The terrace" was a magic word in their locality, conjuring up vistas of air and open spaces, though all you could really see from it was a host of other terraces, pathetic, dirty, with the occasional washing line standing out from the rows of cisterns and heavy piping. So they'd walked talking, and Arjun had been able to discover more in her to attract him than before. Especially her wonderful powers of understanding. . . .

Over dinner, served by the knave-of-all-trades, Raju, who was cook, sweeper, and washerman to the Kumar family, Arjun was moved, not by the intensity of his passion for Rita—which he felt painfully between his thighs—but by its sincerity, which hurt him mainly higher up. He didn't eat very well that night—it's a bit of a handicap when your heart's halfway up your throat—and the occasional contact of her hand when she passed him a dish across the little table meant for four (Kumar never had occasion to invite more than two guests) added sharply to the poignancy of his feeling. Rita, he said to himself over and over again, except when he was dealing with the *rasagollas*, I love you.

When dinner was finished they sat and listened to music—a slightly scratched and infinitely old version of "Does Your Heart Beat For Me," Arjun noted with a deep sense of premonition—while the servant washed up and left. The door clicked shut and the record suddenly came to a stop—a coincidental synchronization that seemed fraught with significance to Arjun: the end of a phase, a tense purgatory with perhaps the promise of better things.

"I've had enough of music," Rita said, getting up to switch off the player. "Let's talk for a while, shall we?"

"Sure—fine," Arjun replied, suddenly flustered despite himself, and getting up too, for want of a better move.

"It's rather uncomfortable sitting out here—shall we go inside?" she asked, and Arjun's heart lurched.

"Yes," he croaked, his throat suddenly dry. She walked normally, almost casually, with the familiar roll of her thickening hips beneath the slightly fading red sari. Yet now, her every step filled him with an overpowering consciousness of her sensuality.

They sat on the bed, looking at each other, and Arjun involuntarily licked his lips in partial dread of what might be coming.

She smiled suddenly, innocently. "So how's your first term in college been?"

The question was so innocuous, so pedestrian, and for that reason, so totally unexpected, that Arjun was momentarily caught off guard. College? First term? Damnitall, was that all she was going to talk about? For a second he was merely surprised, then a flood of disappointment deluged him. The suddenness of the anticlimax was perhaps what got him really hard. First term in college, indeed! And then, a rush of blood to the head—I'll show her. . . .

It happened too quickly for chronicling convenience. Without hesitation, he leaped the gap between him and Auntie Rita and was suddenly on top of her, pushing her onto her back in a spurt of aggressive male dominance that nearly ended in both of them falling off the bed, devouring her in the ardour of his passion as they fought not so much against each other as against the law of gravity.

For her it was more a question of preserving her precipitous balance than her tenuous chastity. To his credit it might be pointed out that he didn't know what he was doing.

Not even when Auntie Rita came up with a series of half-hearted protestations, "No . . . Arjun, we mustn't be doing this. . . . Arjun, really . . . please . . . no, Arjun . . . what will uncle say?"

Even the "What will uncle say" didn't stop him. His heart was already in his mouth and hers in his right hand as lines of half-remembered elegiac poetry ran through his mind, persistent, like some kind of overlapping commentary in a badly produced *Films Division* documentary:

> *If on earth there be paradise of bliss,*
> *it is this, it is this, it is this. . . .*

When he woke up in the morning he was alone, sleeping spread-eagled in sartorial disarray, his hair all over his face and a strangely triumphant feeling ringing in his head. The sound of the shower in the adjacent bathroom permeated his consciousness. Soon afterwards, Auntie Rita—he still couldn't start thinking of her as anything else—appeared, dressed for the day in the customary accoutrements of her sex and standing.

"You can use the bathroom now," she said. He nodded, smiling a trifle apprehensively, not very sure whether she was going to disapprove of him. She smiled in reply, sweet and self-composed again, and walked up to him. "Listen . . . Arjun—about last night. . . ."

"Yes?" his heart was pounding within the aching confines of his ribcage.

". . . don't you have anything?"

"*Don't you have anything?*" The color left Arjun's shocked face as he stumbled backwards in embarrassment and confusion. "*Don't you have anything?*"—but then—then what about last night? Doubt, dread, and gelid fear crept into his mind. But . . . he'd been sure he managed—he had managed, hadn't he? They had— they—had—they had made love, hadn't they? Yet . . . "*Don't you have anything?*" He thought he had, he couldn't be sure, of course, but—was there something more that adults were supposed to have that he didn't or . . .

"I mean a condom, silly. Don't you have anything?" Realization dawned on him like a bucket of cool water suddenly being flung, refreshingly, on his head. (Unfortunate metaphor.) "Oh er no, I'm afraid not," he stammered. "But I'll get one today, Auntie. I . . . I definitely will."

She looked at him, half-amused, very slightly exasperated, and as her luscious lips parted in a smile and he took a hesitant step forward to kiss her, the doorbell rang. "*Namaste*, memsahib . . . it's me, Raju."

And Arjun was left standing in the room, his hands partially stretched out to draw her into an embrace, his mouth still half-open in expectation of delight.

The man seated cross-legged behind the counter, an obese, obscene-looking *lala* in a dirty white *dhoti* and little else, speculatively scratched the three days of stubble on his chin, snarled at no one in particular, and turned to look questioningly at Arjun. To Arjun the look—accompanied as it was by an expressive clawing of the man's corpulent frontal bulge—seemed fraught with accusation, and he hastily averted his gaze from the cardboard Nirodh box behind the glass plate and stared fixedly at the first items of merchandise his eyes fell on.

"You want some of those?" the rasping, businesslike tone of the *lala*'s voice brought Arjun to the sudden realization (this was his week for realizations) that he had been intently contemplating a row of nipples for baby bottles. With a jerk he swiveled around to the shopkeeper, stuttering uncomfortably, "Er—no—no—not at all, thank you." The *lala* accepted his refusal with equanimity, scratched his back, picked his nose, and farted loudly. Overcome by the feculence of the atmosphere, Arjun walked a few hesitant steps away and halted again, uncertain what to do. He couldn't run away from his responsibilities that easily. Damnitall, what was there to be afraid of? He had pictured himself earlier, approaching the solitary *pan*-cigarettes-and-minor-provisions store on the street with a swagger, thumping fifteen paise on the counter and nodding casually at the Nirodh box. The neatly dressed, probably bespectacled salesman would be polite, deferential, respectful, and even perhaps slightly envious of Arjun's looks and apparent sexual status. He would pull out a strip, hand it over to Arjun, who would nod his appreciation, pocket it, and stroll casually away. That had been the general idea, and a pleasantly prepossessing one it had been, too.

Then things had begun to go wrong. To begin with he couldn't find any change, and the prospect of asking for a Nirodh with a ten-rupee note at the corner *dukan* made his heart quail. Perhaps he could buy something else, something worth eighty-five paise, or nine rupees eighty-five paise, or some such, and say casually as the fellow hunted around for change: "Oh, don't bother, throw in a Nirodh to make it a round figure." And the shopkeeper would, of course, comply with gratitude and bless the young fellow's thoughtfulness. Desperately, Arjun had thought of something he might need. A box of chocolates, perhaps? Then the incongruity of the combination—chocolates and a Nirodh—made him do some radical rethinking. Besides, a further thought—after all, this was his next-to-last tenner after buying his return ticket, and he couldn't possibly spend it all on a contraceptive.

Steeling his determination, he had walked, nearly tripping over himself with the uncomfortable sensation that all eyes were on him, to the shop. A few people were lounging about, lighting cigarettes and cracking jokes in Bengali; to Arjun it seemed as if every joke was about him. He was sure they could read the guilt written all over his face; they must be laughing at his transparent ingenuousness. . . . His face flushed as he turned, cheeks burning with shame and guilt and a debilitating sort of fear, and looked around the shop. Through the glass pane he could see a box of the government-subsidized contraceptives, yellow and red and white, the package dominated by some infantile cartoonist's prototype of a happy family (the man's mustache, he noticed, was a northern curler, rather than the pencil-line advertised in Madras) smiling out at him in the carefully measured euphoria of planned parenthood.

Arjun felt far from happy. There was an uncomfortable, rubbery sensation in his legs, and the omnipresence of the *lala* revolted him. The contretemps of the artificial teats did it; he didn't want to stay anywhere near there for another moment. But as he began to walk away, already imagining the whole world's mocking laughter ringing in his reddening ears, second thoughts struck him. Where else could he go? There wasn't another corner store of this type anywhere in the locality. And he had to get the Nirodh; what would Auntie Rita say?

. . . *don't you have anything?*

Arjun plucked up his courage and turned to the shop again. He'd be damned if he was going to muff it this time. He could feel the eyes of all the cigarette smokers burn into his back. So what, let them stare, he told himself defiantly. His face was hot with the flush of shame, and his brow was studded with beads of perspiration. He strode up to the counter and leaned uneasily against it.

"Give me a Nirodh, please," he demanded in a hoarse, sibilant whisper.

"*Kya kaha aap ne?*" the *lala* asked at what seemed to Arjun the top of his voice, straining his ears with the effort of hearing and scratching himself even more profusely.

"A Nirodh, please," articulated Arjun, dying of embarrassment.

"What? What?" By now all eyes were upon them.

Arjun manfully fought the impulse to turn and run.

"Nirodh," he said, softly but clearly, "*ek*—one—Nirodh." He pointed awkwardly but firmly to the box under the glass-pane.

"Nirodh?" the *lala* seemed puzzled. "Oh, *Nirodh*," his face cleared. "No, no, this isn't Nirodh. I keep chewing gum in the box—*Nirodh yahan biklta nahin hai.*"

Arjun gave a deep sigh. To his own surprise, it was one of relief, not agony.

He probably wouldn't have known how to use the damned thing anyway.

When he got back Auntie Rita was finishing her work in the kitchen with Raju.

"Where have you been?" she asked.

"Just went for a stroll," he answered, not very convincingly. She looked up briefly into his face, then looked down at the chopped vegetables again. "Did you get it?"

"Get what?" his studied attitude of innocence at the question betrayed the answer. She looked up at him, into his eyes. He averted his face. "No," he said, his features crumpling.

She smiled. "It doesn't really matter," she reassured him cheerfully. "Now will you please dump all this into that vessel over there while I wash up?"

After lunch they made love again, Raju, who normally slept in the kitchen, having been given the afternoon off. When they finished neither of them dropped off, but lay in each other's arms for a long while. There was a small, contented smile on Auntie Rita's face, and Arjun felt this was the most beautiful moment of his life. *Coitus interruptus* notwithstanding.

"You looked different when you were three," she said, and giggled. The illusion was shattered; seventeen-year-old men lying nude in a woman's arms do not like to be reminded that they'd lain nude in the same arms as sniveling, hollering infants and probably weeweed on them in the process. Arjun felt embarrassed; he'd have preferred to have felt Auntie Rita.

He felt both for the next week, the one inside him, he inside the other; and in the torrid nights and sultry days, they each discovered unsuspected depths in the other. Quite apart from the sex, a curious rapport sprang up between them; a liaison based not on physical intimacy but on a curiously metaphysical understanding. It was beautiful, Arjun often told himself. And his initial vague stirrings of conscience were smothered in their incipience by a line from Somerset Maugham's *The Bread-Winner* that Auntie Rita pointed out to him:

You know, of course, that the Tasmanians, who never committed adultery, are now extinct. . . .

Somehow it was all too good to last, he supposed afterwards, but while he was in Calcutta their idyllic world never looked anything but permanent. The order of their daily lives seemed to fit into some kind of divinely ordained pattern that didn't seem to need change.

Uncle Kumar was to come back the day before the date on Arjun's third-class train ticket, but even his telegram threatening his return and asking to be met at the station was quickly forgotten in Auntie Rita's arms. They laughed, and kissed, and made love, gorgeously wallowing in the luxury of each other's bodies, and Arjun felt a greater joy than he had ever felt in his seventeen years of existence. It was a singularly painless affair, happy, smoothly moving, a sustained, fluffy bed of roses. . . .

Till the last night, when Arjun broached the subject of Uncle Kumar's return. He was lying on her in her bedroom, and he'd just kissed her when he realized the bed wouldn't be free the next day for him to kiss her again. "Uncle Kumar's coming back tomorrow," he said, softly and seriously, looking intensely into her eyes.

She didn't answer; he repeated his statement. "Uncle Kumar's coming back tomorrow," he said, earnestly.

"Mmm," she replied, looking away from him. She made no move to elaborate.

"What'll we do then . . . Rita?"

"Oh, shut up, will you?" she suddenly burst out irritably, turning back with a jerk to look at him. "I know he's coming back, so forget it."

The hurt showed plainly on his face. "I'm—I'm sorry," he said, "I didn't mean to . . . to upset you."

As suddenly, she was contrite. "It's all right, darling," she murmured affectionately, raising her lips to kiss him and nuzzling against his face. "I didn't mean to hurt you either. . . ."

That night their lovemaking was different; gentle, tender, loving in a way he hadn't learned to be with a woman. When it was over, it was morning, and the sun streamed in through the curtains of their bedroom. Kumar was returning that day.

On the way to the station, she said, "Arjun, he mustn't know of this, of anything between us, understand?"

"Of course, Rita," he said.

"Auntie Rita," she corrected him.

He looked at her, searching her face for a hint of a smile. Her eyes were on the road. "Yes—Auntie Rita," he said.

The rest of the day passed in a poignant haze. He couldn't reconcile the Rita he knew with Uncle Kumar's Rita, the wife, the lady of the house, brisk, efficient, dutiful, loyal, loving, doting on her colorless spouse, attending to his every need, ministering to the slightest request with a genuineness of concern and care that should have had the ageing fool's suspicions up if he only hadn't been an ageing fool. Kumar received the red carpet, VIP treat-

ment; wifely hug at the station, chaste kiss from his spouse as soon
as they entered the door, "I missed you very much" all throughout
the car journey, the works.

Through it all Arjun sat, numb and unbelieving, his dismay
and hurt and jealousy writ large on his face.

"What are you looking so gloomy there for, Arjun?" she called
out gaily once or twice while chattering to Kumar, as he sulked on
a dining room chair and watched their marital empathy in action.
He hated Kumar as he had hated no man before, hated his very
guts, hated the impotent, ineffectual old son-of-a-bachelor from
the very core of his being. . . . "Don't be silly, Arjun," she hissed
fiercely at him once when Kumar was out of hearing. "Do you
want him to know what's going on?" And she returned to her
husband, all wifely concern again.

That night Arjun lay alone in bed staring at the ceiling, half
expecting any moment to hear the bathroom door click open, and
her familiar hand on the light switch to flood the room with the
brightness of her smile. But she never came. Inevitable moments
inexorably ticked by. The doors on the other side shut once or
twice, but his never opened. He could hear voices, and, worse,
noises; sounds of love from a throat he had thought was his own.
Finally, as his desperation mounted, he tiptoed to the bathroom
door and listened. . . .

"Ouch!—no, no, darling. . . . My God. . . . Oh, you are a
devil . . ."

There was no mistaking the voice, or the circumstances in
which it was raised. Blindly, he stumbled back to his bed and fell
heavily upon it. His outstretched hand touched and grasped the
small cardboard train ticket that lay on the bedside table, and he
clenched it tightly in his fist, willing it to take possession of him.

It did. The ticket suddenly filled his mind with possibilities,
both symbolic and real. It was a ticket back home, yes, but not
just to the life he had known at home. New worlds beckoned at

the end of the railway line. He grinned at the thought of the well-endowed nymphet. He would be able to handle her now; he knew a thing or two she didn't. And if she failed to work out, well, there would be others.

Arjun smiled in anticipation. This was only the beginning.

1973

The Solitude of the Short Story Writer

There was only one thing wrong with Jennings Wilkes' writing. Verisimilitude.

His stories reeked with it. No one ever accused him of not being true to life, because if anything he was too true to it. He never concocted his plots: he found them in the quotidian experiences of living. He never created characters: he borrowed his friends, and occasionally his enemies, and populated his manuscripts with their likenesses. He never struggled with dialogue; blessed with almost total recall of anything that was spoken to him, he set down others' words as he remembered them. And since in his endeavours he proved unfailingly accurate, lack of realism was never his problem. His stories were overpoweringly realistic.

Needless to say, publishers loved him. Magazines overflowed with his work; scarcely a fortnight passed by without some periodical decorating the stands with yet another Jennings Wilkes short story. Editors would rush enthusiastic letters to him every time a submission came in, and their enthusiasm did not diminish with the passage of time. "There's a fellow who tells it like it is," the portly, cigar-chewing male from the leading women's magazine would affirm to his chief competitor whenever they bought each other grudging lunches at "21." "So *painfully* twue, dear," she would emotively respond. "So painfully *twue.*"

Of course, that was precisely the problem: Jennings Wilkes' fiction was both true and painful, and worse, it wasn't really fiction. The truths he told were about other people, people he knew and associated with—until he committed them to print and they walked out of his life. After beginning his literary career with his popularity indexed in a black leather-bound cornucopia of addresses and telephone numbers, Jennings learned to measure his success by the number of calls he no longer had the courage to make. Each brilliant, honest, revelatory short story proved apocalyptic for some friend, ruined some relationship, shattered some illusion.

Soon his acquaintances began avoiding him, not always subtly. "We don't want to find ourselves splashed across the feature pages of *Harper's Bazaar,*" one couple indelicately informed him when he met them at a restaurant and invited them to join his table. "No, of course you don't," he muttered miserably, retreating to his solitary chair. It was a recurring pattern: sometimes he did succeed in making friends with one individual, only to wreck it all by immortalizing the individual's weaknesses in *Playboy* ("fiction by Jennings Wilkes" the byline read). And the truths he portrayed were painful to him, too: he hated losing his friends.

"Then why do you keep doing it?" an admiring young interviewer from *Writer's Digest* asked him.

"Because," Jennings replied, a spark glowing in his eyes, "because when I meet an individual who interests me I take possession of his character. My mind perceives him as a person, but my imagination gives him a personality. A personality *I* cause to act, to talk, to think, to breathe. And because," he added, his gaze directing the interviewer to his notepad, "Because I have to.

Because creativity is a compulsion and my artistic integrity cannot be compromised, even by my needs as a human being." He watched as the admiring scribe took it all down. Later that evening he penned an acerbic, witty short story (entitled "Naïveté and the Nasty Novelist") about a journalistic ingenue attempting to probe the profound mind of a superior literatteur. *Cosmopolitan* advertised the story on its front cover, and the interviewer admired him no more.

And so, as friends go, his went. They went angrily, occasionally threatening libel, sometimes promising murder, once in a while tight-lipped in seething fury. Some were plainly incredulous. Jennings could never forget one erstwhile friend, waving a copy of *Ladies' Home Journal* at his doorway, pages flapping in righteous indignation: "I can't believe," he had spluttered, "I can't believe you did this." Didn't it matter, the friend went on, that after this their relationship couldn't possibly continue? "Truth is stronger than friction," Jennings responded with a sage smile, before the spine of the magazine's binding struck him squarely on the nose.

"I don't understand it myself, doctor," Jennings said on his second psychiatrist's couch, crossing his feet and steepling his hands in genuinely perturbed introspection. (The first had canceled Jennings' regularly scheduled sessions abruptly after "The Shanks of the Shrunken Shrink" had appeared in *The Atlantic*, a magazine usually available in the doctor's antechamber; "It's not so much the story I mind," Dr. Weingarten had told him, "but the fact that you chose to put it in the *Atlantic*. Do you realize how many of my patients can no longer take me seriously?") "But I can't stop myself—I *have* to write about people I know. And I don't even *want* to stop myself. When I'm sitting at my desk, first thing in the morning, long, yellow sheets of legal-size paper before me, pen and ink by my side—I always use pen and ink, typewriters are deathly for prose—I have an overpowering urge to pick up that pen and put it to those yellow sheets of paper and produce four thousand words of publishable . . . fiction."

"Could you speak up, please?" the psychiatrist asked. "I couldn't hear that last word."

"Fiction," Jennings said, loudly. "I said fiction, Dr. Clausewitz. I *need* to write fiction. Fiction, that is, about those I come into contact with. And I know what you're going to ask me—that's exactly what Dr. Weingarten asked me—you're going to ask me, why does it have to be published? Why can't I fulfill my overpowering urge to write my story and then put it in a paper shredder or something?"

"That's not what I was going to ask you," Dr. Clausewitz said, "but tell me anyway."

"Well, I can't," Jennings replied, shortly. "Publication is important to me. *Communication* is what writing's all about. If my fiction about real people doesn't communicate something to other real people, if it doesn't disseminate the message, the insight, I feel it contains, then the entire purpose of my writing is negated. I need to publish as much as I need to write."

Dr. Clausewitz caressed his goatee. "You haven't answered one question, you know," he said mildly. "Why must you write about other people you know?"

Jennings was stunned by the question, much as a raconteur might be at the end of a joke if asked what the punchline was. "But you don't understand, there's no answer to that question," he mumbled. "That's all I can write about."

Jennings did try to restrain himself on his own. He tried getting up in the morning and *not* sitting at his desk, with its attractions of pen and paper—but he found himself writing in bed, scrawling with a pencil on the blank areas of full-page advertisements in the *New York Times*. He tried shutting himself off from the world so that he would have nothing to write about, but discovered that though shunned by his friends, he was not lacking in attraction for interviewers, autograph-hunters, salesmen, solicitors, would-be authors, and could-be groupies. On the one occasion he succeeded in packing a discreet suitcase and decamping to the wilds of Aspen, Colorado, he was nearly shot by a nightclub entertainer, developed an unpleasant intimacy with the impediments on the ski slopes, and barely avoided double pneumonia after dreaming he was being pursued by one of his not-entirely-fictional characters and jumping in the altogether out of his hotel window into seven feet of accumulated snow. His resultant "Not Quite Altogether in Aspen," rejected by the travel editor of the *National Geographic*, appeared with minor modifications in the *Saturday Evening Post*.

"Not that effective isolation would really do all that much good," Jennings told Dr. Clausewitz as he rested his sore skiing limbs on the analyst's couch and contemplated the ceiling moodily. "I'd probably find myself penning a soul-shattering soliloquy on 'The Privacy of the Persecuted Penpusher.' *And* selling it to *Saturday Review*."

"At least that way you'd only be libeling yourself," Dr. Clausewitz pointed out.

"Don't you believe it," Jennings replied. "One arrives at solitude only by losing the company of, or avoiding, a whole lot of people—so there will always be people responsible for my solitude. And you can bet they'll feature in my—fiction."

Dr. Clausewitz coughed, but let the word pass.

"Why don't you seek some form of diversion from writing?" he asked. "A woman? Several women? Maybe even a man?"

There had always been women in Jennings' life, but none important enough to divert him from his writing. His writing took up most of his day; his women, when he had any, occupied only his evenings and his bed. He encountered no difficulty whenever the urge to write—usually about them—came to him. What female authors have termed "meaningful relationships" became, as a consequence, increasingly hard to come by. His primary fidelity was clearly not to them but to his literary muse, and the few ladies who tolerated Her departed in the wake of such revelatory exegeses as "Sex and the Single Curl" (about the fourth woman in his life, an exquisite if mildly eccentric girl who had a little curl *not* in the middle of her forehead) or "Sinning for her Supper" (about an indigent redhead who had begun to get involved with him, though Jennings was convinced she was more interested in board than in bed).

"How can you carry on a meaningful relationship with an— *individual* who transcribes your bedtime conversation for *Penthouse*?" demanded one lissome brunette as she furiously packed her suitcase. "How can you whisper sweet somethings into the ear of a man you half-expect to respond, 'Speak up, darling—it's ten cents a word?' "

"I guess you're right," Jennings agreed with a morose sigh. "But darling, can't you understand—this is beyond my control. I *have* to write about you. I can't do any—" but the door had slammed shut behind her.

Gloomily, Jennings rose, despairing of his own redemption. A pair of the lady's panties were still on the floor near the bed, omitted in her hasty departure. He rushed to the door with them, shouting as he opened it, "Darling, you've left . . ." He never finished the call; the panties in his mind reminded him irresistibly of the posterior they belonged to, the brunette's only imperfection, a hereditarily heavy derrière whose left half was, despite dieting and exercise, appreciably larger than the right half. His exclamation disintegrated into uncontrollable giggles, and he shut his door again, laughing hysterically while leaning against it.

"Left Behind" appeared in the next issue of *Esquire*.

"Forgive me," Dr. Clausewitz said, leaning forward in his chair, legs crossed at the knee, "but if I may ask a question that is also a suggestion—why do you not, given your obsession with penning the truth, become an investigative reporter instead of a short-story writer? Your—er—talents may then serve a social good, instead of merely contributing to your unhappy state of mind."

"But I already am, doctor," Jennings almost rose from the couch. "Every writer of short stories *is* a reporter, an investigative reporter of society. Besides, it's a question of the appropriate mode of expression. Do you think my perception of feminine foibles, for instance, which is after all what my stories about women depict, would belong on page 1 of the *Washington Post*, under the headline 'Alleged Inconsistencies in Female Behavior Challenged?' And I'm not interested in whether a Third Deputy Assistant Under-Secretary has accepted Swiss currency from a Chilean viceadmiral to help a Cuban megalomaniac kick the bucket. I couldn't write a meaningful piece on that kind of stuff. But if I could have a drink with the Third Deputy Assistant Under-Secretary, and discover that he's cheating on his wife, or that the vice of the vice admiral is the rear of a rear admiral, or that the prospective Cuban bucket-kicker smokes imported Trichinopoly cigars, *then* I could write a fascinating story, suitably garnished, but with the essentials preserved, and that story would *have* to appear as fiction, because that's the mode in which it will receive the kind of readership and the type of attention it deserves."

Part of the problem with Jennings was that he really believed what he said. It is an affliction common to most authors who find themselves theorizing about their art. Writers have as large a capacity for taking their profession seriously as ratcatchers and race car drivers.

"As I see it," Dr. Clausewitz told Jennings at what he announced ("though this has nothing to do with that admirable story in which I fancy I see myself") would be the last session, "your problem is really twofold. On the one hand, you feel impelled to write, but on the other, you can only write about people you know, to their embarrassment and your own discomfiture. Your attempts at resolving this problem have so far dealt primarily with the first part of this dichotomy—curbing your impulse to write. It seems to me it might be more appropriate to endeavor to deal with the second part of it—writing about those you know. By all means, write; certainly, write fiction, or what you consider to be fiction. Try to concentrate your energies, however, on writing not about people you know, but about those you do not. Invent characters. Merge the traits of five people you know into a sixth, nonexistent person—a truly fictional character. Try—"

"You don't know what you're asking of me, Dr. Clausewitz," Jennings interrupted. "You're telling me to betray the very principle of truth I've based my fiction on. If I merge five true characters into one, I lose what is true in all five and create a lie. I can't do it, doctor. I can't."

"Then," said Dr. Clausewitz, looking very old and very tired and very wise, "then do it not as an author but as a human being. Allow one person to matter enough to you—to matter so much to you that you do not want to, *cannot*, desecrate him or her in print. Then—and perhaps only then—will you be able to find your absolution."

Jennings took absolution seriously, "absolutely seriously," as he told the leggy blonde he sat next to on the closest bar stool to Dr. Clausewitz's office (which proved to be, as the doctor had surprisingly indicated with an uncharacteristic twinkle in his eye, seventeen-blocks-and-a-left-turn from the analyst's couch). "Personally, however," he articulated through a thickening tongue, "I prefer salvation in Scotch. Can I buy you a drink, my nebulous nirvana, or are authors and ambrosia off your diet this week?"

The girl laughed, tossing a cultured coiffure. "You're funny," she observed, not entirely soberly.

Jennings stared at her for a moment, digesting the remark. "Yes," he affirmed. "Levity *is* the soul of wit. Will you try a funny fifth of this stuff, or will abstinence make your heart grow fonder?"

"I'll have a vodka," she giggled, toothily. She was a model, all straight lines and elegance, with the kind of high-cheekboned look Faye hadn't entirely dunaway with. ("A model of what?" Jennings joked gauchely. "Charm," came the stunning reply. "The perfume, that is, silly. And a lot of other things besides.") She was young and innocent and what in an earlier age would have been called cutely feminine—the kind of girl who called a spade a thpade. It transpired she had been stood up by the city's leading photographer, and was spending an increasingly aimless wait getting sloshed. Jennings, who found her more than moderately attractive, quickly warmed to her.

"I'm not much of a photographer myself," he found himself saying on his fifth highball (and her fourth vodka), "but why don't we make this meeting *in camera?*"

The girl didn't quite seem to have got it and Jennings wished he hadn't discarded his alternative jokes about darkroom developments and negative answers. He leaned forward and gripped her by the arm.

"Come," he said authoritatively.

She came. Their lovemaking was brief and blurred, as alcoholic amativeness so often tends to be, but she came, shuddering in his arms, and afterwards Jennings lay still, sobered by her sensual elegance, his mind caressing the perfect lines of her mannequin's body. He turned towards her, rolling over onto his belly, and she surprised him by opening her eyes and saying, "Jennings, I love you." The words hit him and he shook her awake abruptly.

"How did you know my name?" he demanded.

She was instantly alert. "Of course I know your name, silly. You're Jennings Wilkes. I've seen your picture in *Playgirl*, with one of your stories—the one about the girl who took drugs, what did you call it—oh, yes, "Methedrine in Her Madness". I recognized you as soon as you sat next to me in the bar. Anyone would." Smiling languidly, she tickled him under the chin and turned back to sleep.

Watching her lying on her side, her graceful curves under his fingertips, Jennings experienced a strange sense of disquiet. *She knew who I was*, he told himself. *She knew all along.* But then why shouldn't she? He did not suffer from any sense of false modesty. His must be a fairly familiar face. Yet the girl, coming so soon after Clausewitz's last disturbing session, seemed too perfectly timed to be true. What was she? A divine gift? A psychoanalytic plant? He shook her awake again.

"What's *your* name?" he asked.

She raised a sleepy hand to touch him. "Cheryll," she said huskily.

"Cheryll Clausewitz?" he was almost barking.

"No, silly, where on earth did you pick that name from? Cheryll Smith."

He felt instantly ashamed. "Go back to sleep, Cheryll," he said softly.

She moved in a week later, by which time they had concluded they wanted each other so much it was pointless living apart. In the meantime, in the few moments he found for writing—since Cheryll demanded more of his time than her few predecessors in residence—he put the finishing touches to a second story about Clausewitz and, inevitably, began one about Cheryll.

"I've got little more than a working title right now, but a lot of empirical data will follow," Jennings explained to Dr. Clausewitz, who had allowed himself to be coerced into restarting the treatment, realizing full well that Jennings needed him only because he had no other friend to talk to. ("If I was Roman Catholic," Jennings had admitted, "I could at least have gone to my father confessor.") "I think I'll call it 'Vodka and the Virgin,' given my penchant for alliteration. And she was, you know, incredibly enough. A virgin. I couldn't believe the stains on my sheet the next morning. Asked her if it wasn't her time of month. She— she—started weeping then," Jennings paused, his brow clouding. "Poor Cheryll."

Poor Cheryll was just what she was—she hadn't proved successful enough a model to be able to maintain herself in the kind of style that successful models could afford and not-so-successful models tried to affect. Jennings, realist that he was, told himself that the saving she would make on her rent had played no small a part in her decision to live with him, and yet the fact that it was *him* she had chosen proved gratifying.

Meanwhile the story progressed. She would occasionally stand over his shoulder while he wrote, give up attempting to decipher his scrawl, and retreat to a magazine or the dressing table; but most of the time she was at a studio, or at several, trying to obtain assignments while he wrote. "Vodka and the Virgin" caused him more trouble than he had expected. Sometimes, the creative demon possessing him, he would write an acidic sentence, only to look up and find Cheryll smiling down at him, a mug of steaming coffee in her hand. She would leave him the beverage and rumple his hair and the spell would be broken. He would score out the sentence in self-reproach.

Somehow, the story moved on.

"She's the only virgin I've ever known, doc," Jennings said reflectively, noting idly that a section of the plaster on the ceiling had begun to crack—it'll peel before next week's session, he thought. "You know, really—the only virgin. Doc, I'm the first man she's ever known. I think about that sometimes when I'm writing, and I tell myself, Jesus, Jennings Wilkes, you can't do this to her. You can't betray a girl who trusts you like Cheryll Smith does, who gives you as much as she has."

"Good," Dr. Clausewitz said. That was all he said throughout the session.

Cheryll in his arms in the living room to a Chopin waltz—biting Cheryll's neck in the kitchen as she garnished an exquisite casserole—Cheryll naked and heaving on the double bed—soaping Cheryll's back in the bathtub—Cheryll smiling and wet and home on the doorstep—writing about Cheryll in the study. The progression always gave him a sense of guilt. Writing was more painful each time he sat down to it, entirely because he could not write beautiful, romantic, adulatory bilge; his perception was too acute and his prose too incisive, even as his preoccupation with her steadily acquired the dimensions of an obsession.

Then, one day, he finished it.

"I've done it, doc," he said in triumph, watching the plaster peel on the ceiling with the quiet satisfaction that comes from the knowledge of inevitability. " 'Vodka and the Virgin' complete and ready for the typewriter. Five thousand intense, painful but brilliant words. It's an affirmation of integrity, of an author's *karma*. Doc, I don't mind admitting to you frankly that there were moments when I thought I wouldn't be able to go through with it. I think I'm beginning to fall in love with her, leggy languor, tumbling tresses et al. There's something so terribly vulnerable in her naïveté—perhaps because her essential simplicity contrasts so strongly with her outward self-possession—that I'm becoming entranced. But you've not been entirely right, doc. She *is* beginning to matter to Jennings Wilkes, the human being—but Jennings Wilkes the author still exults at his completion of her literary exposé. I love the virgin but I've violated her virginity. Don't you see how deep the dichotomy you discerned in me runs?"

"Perhaps," Dr. Clausewitz responded enigmatically. That was all he said throughout *this* session.

Jennings stopped at the bar seventeen-blocks-and-a-left-turn away once more on his way home. It was a strange feeling sitting on her bar stool (the one he had occupied was taken) and then drinking, deliberately, her drink (vodka on the rocks with a dash of lime). Yet Jennings could not define the feeling. He had not come to the bar in quest of anything, not for reminders or assurances or a perverse expiation. Vaguely dissatisfied, he finished the drink and left.

She was due home, he knew, but somehow he did not want to meet her, though he felt impelled to return—to return not to her in the flesh but to her in black ink on yellow paper. He took the elevator to his floor and used the key he had not given her, one that let him directly into his study from the landing. He wanted to be alone with Cheryll there; alone as only an author can be with his creation.

The manuscript was still lying on the table, "BY JENNINGS WILKES" proudly capitalized on the top of the first page. He looked at it and his disquiet lifted. There it was, his story, a tangible embodiment of his perception, his wit, his *power* with the pen. He began to read it, watching, as if from a curiously involved but nevertheless distant vantage point, the words flow across the page, watched them cascade and break in crested waves. He was Neptune, Ahab, Mark Spitz. He was their genesis, their victim, their conqueror. He felt himself caught up in their movement, irresistibly enthralled, felt himself swim in their ambience, sail on their current, rise from their depths. Cheryll's voice, raised outside his study door, broke into his reverie.

"It worked, darling!" The excitement was so foreign to her customary verbal lassitude that Jennings instantly turned his attention to her. She was on the phone in the corridor between his study and the living room, apparently pacing up and down in animation. "He did it, just as you said he would. I came home early today, knowing he'd be away, and sneaked into his study. It's perfect. 'Vodka and the Virgin'—familiar Wilkesian alliteration, establishing the story firmly in the general genre. And the contents—even better than some of his other stuff. I think it's been earmarked for *Elle*. Just wait till this comes out and half of the continental United States will be abuzz with queries about who the 'vertiginous virgin' is. And I'll be up to my ears in modeling assignments!"

There was a pause while the recipient of this breathless analysis responded to it. But Jennings was no longer listening. He strove to focus on the sea of words before him, but found himself drowning in them, their sparkle dulled, his limbs heavy. Clausewitz had been wrong, but *he* had been so much wronger, his perception so pathetically amiss, the truth he had felt compelled to depict now revealed as hollow, tinsel, false. He gripped the sheaf of paper tightly, and then something snapped within him. He was a beached surfer now, watching the foam retreat from the shoreline. The manuscript was ripped apart in two; he watched his hands tear the paper, making no attempt to resist their motion. The story was bisected, and then his hands moved with increasing quickness, and the sheets were torn into furious quarters, the little jagged shreds flying with each fast, flailing violation of their wholeness, till finally no piece was large enough to tear further. He found himself laughing, at first in small sobs, then increasingly uncontrollably, the tears streaming down his face to mingle with the ink on the scraps on the table. With the tears came a greater sense of release than he had ever known, an emptying of the dam-waters through floodgates he had not realized could be opened.

"I'm free!" he shouted, scooping handfuls of shredded story and flinging them into the air, still laughing. "By the Blessed Virgin, I'm free."

He was still laughing when the girl outside finished her telephone conversation.

"Thank you, Dr. Clausewitz," she said.

1977

The Death of
a Schoolmaster

I was ten years old when Achan came into his land. "His" land—how easily one slips into the possessive pronoun. It was Amma's land, not even hers really, but her maternal uncle's. When he'd died heirless, our matrilineal system ensured that Amma inherited his estate. Which meant that Achan, as head of the family, suddenly became a landlord.

I still remember the little, three-room house we were living in when our fortunes so completely changed. There were six of us children then, banging our heads on the low doorway as we crowded into the kitchen for our breakfast *idlis*; only six, because my eldest sister had already been married off a year ago, and my youngest brother was not yet born. We would all sleep side by side on a large cotton mattress spread on the living room floor (or rather, the floor of what I have since come to think of as the living room, a word I had never heard in those days), with a thin sheet to protect us against the mosquitoes. The mosquitoes would buzz around our exposed faces, of course, so that we soon learned to tuck our heads too under the sheet. But all the pulling and the stretching involved in the six of us all keeping ourselves covered meant that often one person at the end got no sheet at all. That was usually my elder sister Thangam, who would curl up quietly on one side without complaint, just as she would forego her own meals in ensuring we all had enough to eat, or miss the bus for school in helping me to get ready for class. And when the sheet gave away one night to some rough tugging by my two elder brothers, leaving a rent down the middle, it was Thangam who slept under the hole, Thangam who saved her next few days' bus fare to buy the needle and thread we didn't have, Thangam who woke up early in the morning to sew the sheet before Achan saw it and beat us all. Those were days when simple sacrifices meant a great deal.

Achan was a schoolmaster then. He was a B.A., an educated man; he could read and write English. The cupboards in our house and in the small room he shared with Amma were crammed with books: advanced English readers, University textbooks, local editions (with impossibly small print) of well-known classics. They were dusty, termite-ridden, cracked and tearing, some without jackets, others carefully wrapped in newspaper covers, the paper yellowing and curling with age, but they were all read. My most enduring memory of Achan in those days is of him in the sagging easy chair on the porch, peering in the light of a kerosene lamp at the torn pages of an aging book. That was before he had come to admit his need for spectacles, or to afford them. Amma would always say he was reading his eyes to ruin, but he would dismiss her with a snort, or ask her to get him a cup of tea instead of bothering him.

Amma was very much the downtrodden wife in those days. When I think of her at that time, I am still startled by the difference between her then and the bustling, vigorous matriarch of later years. Some women grow only in widowhood. As a wife, Amma was quite content to live in Achan's shadow. He had married her, a barely educated orphan with only a prosperous uncle to her name, when she was fifteen. She had known no other brother, or father, or male friend, or instructor, and it was obvious that for her Achan combined all these roles. This didn't mean that she was devoid of individual spirit or conviction, for the children were frequently at the receiving end of her whiplash tongue. It was just that whenever Achan was around, her habitual manner was one of compliant diffidence.

There were so many gaps between them. Age: he was thirty when he married her, double her age, and even as time passed, the fifteen years loomed forbiddingly between them like the shadow of an unscalable cliff. Sex: he was a man in a man's world, equipped to cope with its mysteries; she had gone from the insignificance and fears of a fatherless girlhood into the insignificance and security of an arranged marriage. Education: she had eight grades of schooling, enough to give her a fine, precise, rounded handwriting in the only language she knew, Malayalam; he was the only graduate in the family, a man of learning, steeped in books. The wisdom of age, the assurance of manhood, the knowledge of scholarship, all were his. To these qualities she could only juxtapose her innocence, her uncertainties, her ignorance.

But they were happy together. Happiness can only come when poverty is not equated to want. My father earned only (how easy it is to say "only" now) seventy-five rupees a month for his labors, but he never felt he should want more. Others in the village, many without his B.A., would crowd onto trains and travel long distances to seek clerical jobs in cities like Bombay, which paid them twice as much. They would subsist in hovels and send the bulk of their earnings home to their families in Kerala. A neighbor once wondered aloud whether Achan too could not do better by taking the typing course offered in the next town and going to work as a stenographer in Bombay like so many husbands and sons of her acquaintances. The vehemence of his reaction rapidly established for her and anyone else who might have been listening (as I was) that neither the skill nor the profession concerned was worthy of a gentleman's consideration. In any case, it never crossed Amma's mind to urge any change upon Achan. He was what he was, and it was her duty to serve him and raise his family. That was enough for her.

When the inheritance came they were caught off guard. I suppose they must have known, in some recess of their minds, that Valiamaman's assets would one day be theirs, especially as the years went on and he failed to acquire or produce other heirs. But Amma was not the kind of person to think very much about it and Achan had no place for such prospects in his world of books and school papers. I imagine that, in any case, they were not expecting anything quite so soon. Valiamaman was an active sixty at the time of his sudden death in circumstances which were never satisfactorily explained to us children. Later inquiry and surmise have led me to conclude he had a seizure when closeted with the buxom young maidservant whom Amma dismissed soon after we moved in. He was an energetic man to the end.

The move was traumatic. It meant a major displacement from our little town, where Achan taught at the government high school, to our ancestral village over fifteen miles away. It meant changing the habits of a lifetime, bus schedules, games, friends. It meant coping with the mysteries of a thirty-five-room house where suddenly each of us had our own bedroom-cum-study. We could never come to terms with this unwanted gift of privacy and would end up, as before, sleeping side by side on our cotton mattress in the grand front room where Valiamaman used to receive the visits of his fellow *zamindars* in more prosperous times.

And for Achan it meant the unfamiliar responsibility of sixty acres of paddy fields, scattered over two villages forty miles apart. His land.

He had to give up the school. For one thing he was no longer down the road from it. He would have had to walk nearly an hour, catch an unreliable bus and walk ten minutes again, none of which would have been good for either his dignity or his feet. For another, he had to keep an eye on his land, attend to details of its ploughing, sowing, irrigation, and harvesting, employ contract labor, pay the government levies, apply for fertilizer, arrange for the sale of the produce. It was a full-time job.

It was also too much for him. I don't know when I began to realize it, but it became apparent before long that Achan couldn't cope. He would return from a hot, dusty day in the fields, exhausted and irritable. He would delve suspiciously into the dinner Amma laid out for him, and complain uncharacteristically about the vegetables in the *avial* or the sourness of the *thayiru*, bark at a few of us, and attempt to seek solace in his easy chair. But no sooner had he turned a page of whatever book he had picked up than someone would emerge on the veranda, hands folded in supplication, to raise some problem about the land. And Achan would put his book down in despair and try to arrive at a decision on some matter he knew less about than his visitor.

It was obvious, too, that Achan's lack of aptitude for farming was taking its toll on the family finances. We children were never encouraged to think about money, an inhibition which in the past hadn't prevented us from realizing we hadn't any. But Amma let us know early on that if we had come up in the world to possess the largest house in the village, with our own mango tree and vegetable garden, we didn't have much other than some tumbledown furniture to go with it. We grew more or less whatever we needed to eat, but money for everything from clothes to bus fare had to come from the sales of our paddy, and Amma made it clear there wasn't very much of that after salaries and levies had been paid and the upkeep of the house attended to. Under Achan's management the returns from the farm seemed to decline. The telltale signs appeared in the weeks when the profits from the previous harvest had dwindled and the expenses for the new sowing began to mount. At these times, our milk would turn watery, the clothes would be given less often to the washerwoman, a special occasion would no longer be celebrated by a bullock cart trip to the movie theater in the nearest town.

It was during one of these periods that Thangam fell ill.

Thangam, who helped Amma do without a full-time servant by working in the kitchen before and after school; Thangam, who attended to everything from my scraped knee to the weekly puja offerings; Thangam, who silently bore the brunt of Achan's irrational anger for anything that had gone wrong in the house; Thangam fell ill, and it was as if our world had collapsed around us. She stumbled one day in the kitchen, dropping a precious pan of boiling milk in her fall to the floor, and it was more the spilt milk than the fall that convinced me something was seriously wrong. Amma ran in alarm and anger to her, but after one look at Thangam's face she brought the hand she had raised for a slap gently down upon her daughter's forehead. I was in the kitchen by then, and I could see the alarm on her face.

"You're very hot, my child," she said quietly. "You have a fever."

"Nonsense, mother, it's just the heat of the kitchen," Thangam retorted, but in a voice so weak I knew she was lying.

"Go and lie down, my dear," Amma said. "I can manage in here." And despite Thangam's protests she was bundled off, with me in tow.

When Achan came home that night he was initially too wrapped up in his problems to notice that anything was amiss. Then it struck him that it was I who was helping my mother serve his dinner. "Where's Thangam?" he asked. "Has she already gone to sleep?"

"No, she is not well, poor child," Amma replied. "She had a fever and I've asked her to lie down."

"What have you given her? Has she eaten anything?"

"No, she didn't want any food."

"Medicine? Did you give her something for the fever?"

"I didn't know where you kept the medicine. I thought I would wait for you to come."

Father washed his hands and went to Thangam. She was shivering uncontrollably under the thin sheet. Drops of perspiration stood on her brow like beads fallen off a broken chain.

"You should have called a doctor," he said accusingly to Amma.

"How could I? I don't even know where to find one or what his name is. I waited for you to come," she repeated despairingly.

"It's too late for tonight. Tomorrow, the boy must go to Dr. Parameshwar in Nemmara." He gave me instructions on how to get to the doctor's clinic in the nearby town. "Ask the doctor to come here."

"But how can we possibly afford to pay. . . ?" my mother began.

"I'll find a way," Achan said grimly. "Get the doctor. I have to go early tomorrow to our fields in Shoranur. I may not be back till very late. If the work keeps me too long and I cannot get a bus, it could even be tomorrow afternoon before I return. But don't worry. I am sure the doctor will take good care of Thangam."

I slept next to my sister that night. Her skin was so hot I recoiled from her in shock. She dozed fitfully, her body racked by shudders. Occasionally she cried deliriously in words I could not understand.

In the morning I ran through the rice paddies to the nearest bus stop. It took me twenty minutes on a normal morning; today I did it in ten. There I waited in an agony of frustration for the bus to Nemmara. When it came it was full, but I clambered onto the tailboard and clung on in desperation throughout the bumpy ride. My father's directions were good; I found the clinic without great difficulty. There were a number of patients in the line and in the waiting room. I tried to barge in to see the doctor but was sharply reprimanded by a nurse. Each moment seemed to drag by until finally I was ushered into the doctor's chamber.

"My-sister's-very-sick-you-must-come-and-see-her," I burst out in one breath.

The doctor laughed. He was a kindly man, with a round face and a bushy, black moustache. "Now, now, hold on there a minute, son," he said. "What exactly is the matter with your sister?"

I told him. His face became grave. "Yes, I think I must see her," he agreed. "Can you bring her here?"

"But it's impossible!" I expostulated. "She can hardly sit up. And we—could not bring her in our bullock cart." I did not add that we could not afford a taxi from the town.

He reflected for a moment. "All right, I shall come," he said finally. I can still remember the sense of triumph and relief which his words produced in me. "But not just yet. I have all these patients to see." He gestured towards the line outside.

"But you must come now," I pleaded stubbornly. "My sister cannot wait."

"She will have to," he said firmly. "These people have all been waiting."

"But this is different! She may—she may—die." I whispered the last word, confronting its horror for the first time.

He looked at me in exasperation.

"I shall not leave this room till you agree to come with me," I said very quietly.

He came, his anger dissolving in tolerant laughter. And Thangam didn't die. When we got home, I saw to my surprise a familiar figure sitting by Thangam's bedside, stroking her hair. My father.

He didn't say a word in response to my look of astonishment. But after the doctor had examined Thangam, administered his medication, told us all would be well in a few days and left us with his prescription, my father explained what he had decided to Amma.

"I came back," he said simply, tousling my hair and sounding defensive. "And I'm not going to go again. It is madness, traveling all the way to Shoranur every other day. And it is not as if my going there makes a lot of difference either. My place is here, with you and my children. Balan Nair, your Valiamaman's old retainer, has offered to manage these fields for us. He will give us a specific portion of the harvest, and attend to all the daily chores. It will save us a lot of trouble."

"But—how can you give it all to him?" Amma was incredulous. "More than half our land is there, in the Shoranur fields."

"I'm not *giving* anything to him, woman," Achan rejoined irritably. "The land is still ours. He is just going to run it for us, that's all. And I can keep an eye on the smaller fields around our village. Nathan is old enough to help me." Nathan was my oldest brother. It was obvious he was not going to amount to very much at school. My father had clearly made a wise decision.

Things got a lot better after that. Balan Nair took complete charge of running the fields, and though later his dues were paid at intermittent intervals and he increasingly seemed to have new reasons for not giving Achan all that we expected, we still had an assured income without Achan having to lift a finger for it. I still remember Balan Nair's frequent visits to Achan, a clean white cloth flung over one shoulder, his head bending so low in respect over his folded hands it looked as if he was going to drink from them. Achan was happy and relaxed. He had more time for his books now as Nathan gradually took over control of the closer fields. My brother had that capacity to alternate between seasons of hectic activity and periods of enforced idleness that in our country characterizes the rustic life. Achan was able to leave virtually everything to him—and, of course, to Balan Nair.

This left Achan a lot more time for me. He would let me into his "book-room," as we children called it, and turn a casual browse into a magic world of instruction and enlightenment. He taught me, without the drudgery of a classroom, things I would never have been able to learn in school. He introduced me to the English language, to the pleasures of literature and the perils of philosophy. When he caught me straying into a card game with my brother's farmer friends, he would pull me out on some pretext and shame me with his disapproval. As to the new vocation the inheritance had given us, Achan never let me have anything to do with it. The first time I attempted to accompany Nathan *etta* to the field, he stopped me. "That's not the world I want you to inhabit," he said to me fiercely. "Leave the fields to your brother, you understand? And never let me catch you going there again." His interdiction was so total I was the only male in my family who didn't know the way to our *kalam* from the house.

The years passed in tranquility. Thangam, restored, already an able housewife in her teens, was married to the son of a landed family. Achan did not have to borrow for the dowry, as he had had to do for my eldest sister. Another child was born, my youngest brother, the only birth in the big house. The event seemed to signify a rebirth for Amma too. She began to acquire more authority in her role, as Achan slipped more and more into complaisance. I did very well at school and was admitted to the government Victoria College in Palghat, the district capital thirty miles away. It was clear I was the one destined to follow in Achan's educated footsteps.

Those were turbulent years in Kerala. All the big issues of the day seemed to be emerging in the microcosm of our little state—communism versus bourgeois democracy, parliamentary politics versus revolution, capitalism versus socialism, free education versus scholarly privilege, agrarianism versus industrialization. Tempers heated rapidly on our campuses: conflicts erupted over words and were fought over bodies. I was caught up irresistibly in the mood of the times. I had the talents of a "leader": a loud voice, a way with words, and a willingness to employ both in the service of my interests. I joined an opposition party and rose rapidly in it. Before long, while I was still in my mid-twenties, I was awarded the party's ticket to contest the elections to the state assembly.

I went home in a mood of jubilation to prepare my campaign. It was there that the first news of misfortune reached me. Achan had developed some sort of a mysterious pain that left him virtually crippled. The local doctors seemed to be able to do nothing to relieve his discomfort, and could only attribute it to a particularly severe form of rheumatism.

I wanted to help, but I was too much in the fray of my political battle. I left it to my brothers to investigate the matter further, and embarked upon my electioneering.

I had early arrived at a populist brand of politics, which suited my rhetorical style and my ideological convictions. My familiarity with the ideas of equality and freedom had first come from the crumbling pages of Tom Paine, Mill, and Rousseau on my father's bookshelves. But I had been able to update their ideas by the inevitable university acquaintance with Marx and a diligent reading of Nehru. Today I spoke eloquently against priests and businessmen, and for free schooling and land reform. The latter was an issue that rapidly caught the imagination of my predominantly rural constituency. "Land to the people!" I declaimed. "The tillers must benefit from their toil! Down with the landlord exploiters!"

My popularity was rapidly achieved. There was I, the educated, city-college product of a good family, speaking up for the people's rights. My father had instilled in me the view that ideas were unrelated to life: they inhabited a rarefied world of books, not of men. "You are what you believe, my son," he would often say. Since philosophy was a diagnosis, not a prescription, for life, beliefs did not have to be reconciled to behavior. The country's most prominent communists were themselves prosperous elitists. I thus saw no contradiction between my convictions and my context; I thought I was merely going one step further by translating my views into votes. And I did it well. With my oratorical skills I was able to give expression to the inarticulate grievances of the landless peasant. His work would be rewarded, I promised. Land would go to the tiller. There would be a ceiling on how much property one person could own.

I received the news of my victory at the polls the same evening as the laboratory reports came in on my father. Achan had cancer. His pains would never disappear.

I can remember the shock. I can recall the euphoria. I am no longer sure whether one succeeded in crowding out the other.

Achan was dying while I was to attend my first session of the state legislature. "Go, my son," he said to me when I turned to him in anguished farewell. "I am proud of you. You and what you stand for represent the future. Do not hold it up for the past."

Achan was flown to Bombay, where my eldest sister and her husband lived, for specialist treatment in a cancer hospital. I promised to go there as soon as I could complete my first major task at the assembly. It was the Land Reform Bill. I was one of its prime movers.

When I got to Bombay the news was all bad. Achan's cancer had made alarming progress. Only prolonged and expensive treatment, using equipment and medicine that would have to be flown in from abroad, could forestall the inevitable. There seemed to be no way we could afford that.

"But we can," said Amma excitedly. "We *can* afford it. All we have to do is sell the land we've let out to Balan Nair. We don't need it any more. Almost all the children are settled—we can live off the fields in our own village. Why, we can probably sell the land to Balan Nair himself."

I agreed, and volunteered to rush back to Kerala to arrange the transaction.

Balan Nair received me in his house. As I stepped across the smooth, new, cement pathway into the freshly painted coolness of his living room, I realized with a shock why his payments to Achan had been so irregular. He had clearly done very well out of the arrangement.

"New house?" I couldn't resist asking as he ushered me to a chair.

"Built it last year," he admitted proudly. "We have had a few good harvests." He sat, too, on a slightly higher chair, and then it struck me: with my father he had always stood.

"It is about those harvests that I have come to speak to you," I said awkwardly, accepting a servant's proffered cup of tea. "As you may know, my father is not very well."

"I have heard," he replied. "Very sad news." He didn't sound sad at all.

"Achan requires some specialized treatment in Bombay, which is going to cost a lot of money," I began. I paused, not knowing exactly how to phrase it.

"Have you come to me for money?" he asked abruptly.

"Of course not." I could feel the color rising to my cheeks. "I have come to tell you that we wish to sell our land here in Shoranur. That is the only way we can raise the funds we need to pay the hospital."

"Very interesting." Balan Nair said, flicking absently at a passing fly with the loose end of his shoulder-cloth.

"I thought you might be interested, perhaps, in purchasing it." I cast a look around the evident prosperity of his surroundings. "I am sure you can afford it, and we will of course arrange a fair price."

"I would be very interested indeed," Balan Nair replied, "If you had any land to offer me in Shoranur. But I didn't know you owned any land here."

At first I thought he hadn't understood. "You know the land I mean," I said a trifle impatiently. "The land my father let you use, here."

"I know no such thing," Balan Nair responded equably. And then it hit me. He was going to deny the arrangement had ever existed.

"You mean . . ." I spluttered, rage battling incomprehension.

The words wouldn't come; they tripped over barriers of confused thought and fell soundlessly in my mind.

"I mean that the land I use here is mine," he said. "I have tilled it for the last fifteen years. Last week I registered my possession of it, quite legally, under the new Land Reform Act. I believe you know something about the Act?"

The question rendered me speechless. I had never associated the Act with him. Land reform, in my mind, had nothing to do with the likes of Balan Nair. It was an idea redolent with images of half-naked laborers, the sweat glistening on their black muscular bodies, their voices raised in a raucous clamour for justice. Balan Nair didn't fit the concept, or the cause.

"Land to the tiller. Tenancy rights. A well-drafted piece of legislation, that. You must read it sometime." The white teeth, the white shoulder-cloth, mocked me in their triumphant brightness. "It provides for a ceiling of twenty acres per person, provided the land is actually used by the owner. I have registered twenty acres in my name, eighteen in my wife's. We propose to continue to cultivate this land. *Our* land."

He gestured to the maidservant to fill up my cup. I thought of his hired laborers outside, bending in the sun over the ruts in the fields. Land to the tiller: the slogan had found its reality.

"I believe you know, better than most people, that it would be futile to make an issue of this," he added. "You wouldn't stand a chance in any court of law." He smiled indulgently at me. "And now, is there any *other* land you would like to sell. . . ?"

Though I knew it was hopeless, I tried to have something done. I called up lawyers, spoke to officials, even tried to press some of my political connections into service. In the end I realized what I should have known all along: nothing could be done. Change had come, and it was immutable. The law, and justice, were on Balan Nair's side.

Achan came home from Bombay. I had offered to take a loan which I could pay back later, but he had refused to hear of it. I tried to persuade Amma to take it, but she was too proud. If their land could not pay for Achan's treatment, they would do without it. I accompanied them back home in a torment of guilt and self-reproach.

Achan died slowly, his pain eased by stronger and stronger tranquillizers. In one of his last few lucid moments, he whispered hoarsely into my ear as I leaned my head towards his gaunt and shrunken face. "Have no regrets, my son," he said. "I don't have any. My time has come. The foreign treatment would only have prolonged my pain. Do not blame yourself about anything. What you did was what you believed in. Do that always, and you will always be right."

He died later with a book in his hands, trying through the blurred mists of his suffering to read some well-worn truth, reinforce another belief. I was there to slip the volume from his hands and gently close his tired eyes. I knew that, thanks to him, mine would always be open.

1981